About the Author

Cassie has always had a passion for writing and tends to read any book she can get her hands on. As a child, she dreamed of discovering Narnia in her closet and secretly prayed that Peter Pan would come fly her away to Neverland. Her imagination never left her, and when she's not busy fantasizing, she's busy planning what story to write next. She writes from her home in Maine but one day hopes to write from around the world.

Palace of Power: Story of Sparta

Cassie Claremont

Palace of Power: Story of Sparta

Olympia Publishers
London

www.olympiapublishers.com
OLYMPIA PAPERBACK EDITION

Copyright © Cassie Claremont 2024

The right of Cassie Claremont to be identified as author of this work has been asserted in accordance with sections 77 and 78 of the Copyright, Designs and Patents Act 1988.

All Rights Reserved

No reproduction, copy or transmission of this publication may be made without written permission.
No paragraph of this publication may be reproduced, copied or transmitted save with the written permission of the publisher, or in accordance with the provisions of the Copyright Act 1956 (as amended).

Any person who commits any unauthorised act in relation to this publication may be liable to criminal prosecution and civil claims for damage.

A CIP catalogue record for this title is available from the British Library.

ISBN: 978-1-83543-490-1

This is a work of fiction.
Names, characters, places and incidents originate from the writer's imagination. Any resemblance to actual persons, living or dead, is purely coincidental.

First Published in 2024

Olympia Publishers
Tallis House
2 Tallis Street
London
EC4Y 0AB

Printed in Great Britain

Dedication

I dedicate this book to the most powerful woman I know; my mother, Cathy Cleaveland.

A Note from the Author

The names of characters within the story are depicted from Ancient Greece and Greek Mythology. Please note, there are many ways to say these names, and I have chosen to pronounce them as written below. You may pronounce them as you wish or pronounce them as I have in the key provided.

King Eurotas: (Your-row-t-as)
Amyclas: (Am-ee-class)
Queen Clete: (Kl-ea-t)
Eurydice: (Your-rid-is-ee)
Princess Sparta: (Sp-ar-ta)
Zosime: (Zo-sim-ee)
Princess Tiasa: (Tea-a-za)
Theron: (Th-are-on)
Taygete: (Tay-jet)
Zeus: (Zoo-s)
Poseidon: (Po-side-on)
Lacedaemon: (L-ace-day-mon)
Basilius: (Base-ill-ios)
Callias: (Kal-eye-as)
Kleon: (Klee-on)
Nicander: (Nick-and-er)
Lysander: (Lie-sand-er)
Nerissa: (N-ar-is-a)
Sophus: (So-fuss)
Philo: (File-o)

Helene: (Hell-ee-n)
Apollonia: (Apple-o-knee-a)
King Erysichthon: (Air-ee-z-ich-don)
General Adamantios: (Adam-ant-ee-os)

Respect earns you loyalty.
Loyalty gets you followers.
Followers become an army.
An army makes you a leader.
A leader becomes a king.
A king becomes a God.

Chapter I

From the time I was little, I cannot remember any choice that was ever my own. I had to walk, speak, wear and obey everything I was told to do. I was the king's daughter after all, and while it seemed like a blessing, to me it felt like a curse. I should be thankful to live such a life as I've seen the life others live. The difference is, I am royalty and they are not, but they are free and I am not.

Like a bird in a cage, I was to remain inside the palace's walls. The word of my beauty had reached beyond the seas and throughout the kingdoms of Greece. My father had offers for my hand in marriage since the day I was born. "A girl as bright as the burning sun and as radiant as its rays." Those were the words my tutor repeated to me when I was able to learn how to read and write. She told me, "Someday, a man whom my father finds worthy will have my hand in marriage, and any man the king finds worthy is a man worthy of me."

I detested her words silently, and when I bled for the first time, it signified my fertility. I was no longer a child but a young woman who was coming of age. It was with this information that my father went on a rampage in search of a man worthy of marrying his daughter, the princess of Laconia. I always thought that I would be free to choose the man I would marry, but my father had found a man he grew fond of, Lacedaemon.

Lacedaemon was a handsome young man, I was told. He was the son of the great god Zeus and Pleiad nymph Taygete. A strong man who was charming, friendly, stoic, and intelligent. However, he was twice my age, and I was arranged to marry a man I had never met before.

I suppose that's why I ran away. The impenetrable walls that were the Kingdom of Laconia could not hold me anymore, and I would race to reach the sea without being caught. I was tired of having everyone make and decide my life for me. For once, I wanted to make my own choices and live my own life.

The light of the moon glowed from above, and I could smell the salty air in my nose. I had snuck past the guards with ease and knew the sequence of their rounds of patrol. I timed it perfectly, and when I reached the empty court yard, I scaled the vines of the wall and quietly leapt over it. The thick bushes and foliage were enough to camouflage me from the guards, and I moved with the shadows past them.

I made an effort to blend in with the darkness and move quietly and carefully. I didn't want to get caught. If I did, tomorrow I'd be wed to a man I hadn't even met yet. I'd be sent to live with him in another kingdom, or a part of Laconia, and remain there forever. That was not my wish; it was my father's, and I was not about to let it come true.

I made it down to the port, where the ocean waves sparkled under the moon's gleaming light and the stars shimmered from above. I found a small fishing boat and released it from the dock. I had heard stories of sailing and adventures from the guards. I eavesdropped on their conversations when I was supposed to be studying various passages of literature.

I had no clue how to use a boat, but I would have to figure it out. My freedom depended on it. I knew the moment someone realized that I was missing, the search for me would be vast. The entire kingdom would be in dismay, and my father would leave no stone unturned until I was found. The Great King Eurotas was a man of power and diplomacy. He had known the scars of battle and the sacrifices it took for peace. I knew his decision to drain Laconia's swamp lands and create rivers was one that benefited our kingdom greatly. I suppose that's why some refer to him as "the river god" and even call the river "Eurotas" after him.

I jumped in the small boat and began fumbling with the oars like I'd seen men do in the past. I would watch them out of my window in the palace and had seen their arms move forward and back, clasping each oar in hand. I began that paddling motion, and soon the dock became but a small dot in my vision as I was far out to sea.

The breeze rippled through my cloak, and I felt the mist touch my soft skin. I did not stop rowing as I knew I could make it to my destination if I tried hard enough. I had never been there before, but I had heard stories of my father and mother visiting that island of tranquility. I hoped I could hide there long enough to somehow figure out a plan to get farther away and disappear.

For now, I thought of myself and the life I was leaving behind. Would the gods be disappointed and interfere with my will to flee? Would a sea monster be sent to eat me? Would Zeus be mad that I was running away from wedding his son? I hoped that the gods might see things my way and let me have my freedom. Yet, the thought of them watching me and questioning or interfering with my plans was always on my mind.

I must think of other things, I thought to myself. I began to wonder what my sister Tiasa would think of me running away. We were close because we shared the same blood, but more often than not, we were distant. I was angry as to why my father wasn't off playing "match maker" with her first but rather with me.

I always considered her more beautiful than myself, and beauty seemed to be a quality I was unable to see within me, no matter how often I was told otherwise. I rather saw myself for my intellect and ability to propose bright ideas that were often shut down. I even saw myself as a warrior, perhaps? I know it was not my place, but I liked the way the guards and soldiers fought.

I found myself wanting to jump into the colosseum just for the thrill of it; to feel what fear the warrior must be feeling, or maybe not fear at all, but rather anticipation for what mighty beast he may slay next. I loathed at the chance to feel excitement like that running rapid through my veins. My outings to watch the fights were often all that kept me sane. More often than not, I was stuck in the palace, studying whatever scripture was placed in front of me.

Tiasa studied too, but she had more freedom than me. She flirted with the guards and even courted a few. I was sure my father knew of this, but he didn't seem to care. All eyes were on me at all times, and I was all anyone could seem to pay attention to. I was guarded, protected, fed, washed, bathed, tutored, and dressed, and each moment of every waking day consisted of no privacy. It was only when I slept and was left alone in my dreams that I felt relief. Though, there were still guards pacing outside my doors each and every night.

How I had proudly snuck past them, and how I was now on a journey of my choosing, free at last. Princess Sparta of Laconia was no more; in this boat, I was just Sparta, the free.

Chapter II

I continued rowing until I felt my arms would fall off. I looked up at the sky to see the moon still shining from above, and the stars still shimmering. The reflection of sparkles mirrored off the water, and I felt like I was wading in a sea of stars as I drifted, letting the waves take me to my hope-filled destination.

The sun would be up soon, and I knew I had to make it there before dawn if I didn't want to be seen by any oncoming or passing ships. I could see the mist begin to turn into fog as it floated past my boat. I kept rowing and squinted my eyes toward the distance. I could make out what looked like a giant whale in the middle of the ocean, but I knew it was no whale; it was the island of Cythera.

I jumped up with excitement, nearly falling overboard. I grabbed the paddles and continued rowing toward that large land mass. I could see the moon beginning to fade back into the darkness of which it came from, and the stars seemed to follow it back into hiding. The sun had awoken, and slowly, its rays began to emerge through the clouds in streaks.

The waves turned from dark blue into a light and cheery color of turquoise. I could see the rocky coast and sandy beaches aligning the bay of Cythera. The trees swayed in the wind, and I could see their palms frolicking in the breeze. I smiled, knowing I had made it, and I was one step closer to freedom.

I came upon a desolate stretch of sandy beach that was bare but beautiful. I rowed until I felt the boat hit the patch of sand and hopped out of it, holding my dress and cloak, careful as to not get them wet. My feet hit the water, and I felt the warm sand wrap around my toes. I smiled and began venturing up toward a grove of palm trees.

I found some coconuts and banged them against a sharp rock to plunge a hole into the tough husk of the nut. I lifted it to my lips and drank the cool liquid that poured down my throat refreshingly. I then banged the coconut harder on the sharp rock, and it split open in two. I pried the white fruit from its shell and began eating it contently.

I stood carrying fruit in one hand and a tall stick I had found in the other. I made my way through the thicket of the jungle and admired the blooming flowers of pink and yellow on my journey to find the port of Cythera. I trekked for some time and began to hear water rushing violently.

I came upon a waterfall that flowed effervescent liquid which was colored sky blue. The water gushed into a pool below, and I stood on the rocks, peering below into the hole that caught the water. I ditched my stick and coconut. I threw off my clothes and jumped into the pool of water below. I hit the water with a "splash," and the coldness of it consumed me quickly, but I felt refreshed, awakened by the glorious waters.

I found myself floating and looking up at the sky, covered with cotton white clouds. The water moved my body in a circle, and I smiled with the feeling of freedom. I swam toward the rocks and lay on them, allowing the sun to dry me before I hiked to retrieve my dress and cloak.

I dressed quickly and ventured on. I came upon a small cliff and could see the port a ways' away. *Would anyone recognize me?* I thought, and I knew that most likely since no one had ever seen me before, I was safe. I was rarely allowed outside the palace's walls and, in a way, it would be a blessing. I could easily blend in, and I hoped I'd find someone who could take me far away from Laconia and to someplace new.

After some hours, I finally reached the port. I was exhausted but glad. I kept my hood down and walked through the people crowding the docks. Many had set up small displays of wooden crates or clothed tables, anxiously awaiting Cythera's visitors to come and make a purchase from them. Fish, crabs, woven clothes, finely crafted and embroidered blankets, even jewelry was displayed for all to see. This place seemed to have everyone selling something of every kind.

I looked around admiring all of the goods but quickly realized through the glances of others that I was not someone normal. I was different, and I kept my gaze lowered as to not raise suspicion. I politely came upon a boat captain and lightly tapped on his shoulder. He turned around and said, "May I help you, Miss?"

"Apologies for bothering you, but I was wondering if you know of any ships that are setting sail for some place far away from here?" I asked politely.

"Most every ship here is from faraway. What is it you're running from?" he asked suspiciously.

"Doesn't matter if I'm willing to pay for passage," I replied blatantly.

The man smirked and looked at me before saying, "There's a boat that's leaving for Ithaca as soon as the sun rises tomorrow morning. Meet me here, and we'll get you aboard."

"Thank you," I replied to him as he turned away to continue tying knots in rope. I walked away eagerly and found a stone wall at the edge of the dock, meeting the sea. I climbed onto it and sat there, watching the boats come into the bay. I hoped none would be my father's, or any Laconian official for that matter.

I saw a small tree bearing tangerines and reached over to grab a couple. I peeled the fruit and tossed the peels into the waves. In the distance, I heard bells ringing, people shuffling and talking amongst themselves or to others. I could hear the wind rustling the leaves of the trees and ripping through sails of ships and boats. I smelled fish being cooked and could see small fire pits where women rolled bread over and over again.

I sat there, taking it all in, and breathed a breath of relief. It was by now that I knew the palace would be in a frenzy, looking for me, and the search would begin quickly. I only prayed that no one figured out that I had come here, and by tomorrow morning, I would be well on my way to Ithaca. Well, on my way to the freedom I had always dreamed of having.

I heard a loud noise and saw that a young boy had dropped a barrel of fish that spilled all over the dock. He was scolded harshly by one of the fishermen, and I watched as he got slapped in the face. The boy looked ashamed and quickly began curdling the fish back into the barrel as fast as he could.

I watched as he struggled to once again lift the barrel, and it was now slippery, which made the task all the more difficult. I climbed off the wall and walked up to him as he placed the barrel to the side of a building. I didn't say anything, but instead, held out my hand, offering him a tangerine.

Chapter III

Kingdom of Laconia

The palace walls shook as the guards rushed up and down frantically. The maids were searching every room and every crack as to where I could be. My father stormed up and down the halls as my mother followed behind him quickly. Her lavender-colored gown flowed with her pace, and she became more concerned at each remark of my father's facial expressions that only grew with worry as he winded down the halls farther and faster.

"She has to be here somewhere!" King Eurotas shouted.

"Could she have been taken?" Queen Clete asked.

"May the gods have mercy," he replied to her angrily, marching forth and into the throne room. The room was wide and vast. Its stone pillars and great design left an artistic touch fitted for royalty.

"Silence!" King Eurotas yelled, waving a hand before sitting on his throne. Queen Clete stood behind him, trying to look at ease, but all she conveyed was worry. Tiasa stood on the other side of King Eurotas and looked just as concerned.

"Your Majesty, we have no leads as to where the young princess may be," a nobleman said, stepping forward.

"Then find one!" King Eurotas yelled back before placing his face into his hand.

"King Eurotas," General Adamantios said.

"Please tell me, Adamantios, that you have something, anything, as to where she is."

"I believe that someone in the palace knows something of her whereabouts. There is no way that Princess Sparta could have left without help."

"You believe someone has betrayed us?" King Eurotas asked, shifting his anger to rage.

"Unfortunately, I do, Your Majesty," General Adamantios replied.

"Then find out who, and bring them to me."

"Yes, Your Majesty."

General Adamantios left with haste and with soldiers at his side. He gave swift instructions to round up every person in the palace for interrogation. The soldiers began grabbing maidens, tutors, cooks, seamstresses, artists, scribes, and anyone who served the palace or had any reason to be in it.

King Eurotas sat on his throne, huffing with anger, but inside, he felt a great sadness for the loss of his daughter.

"She was so young, only thirteen! What would someone possibly want with her?" Tiasa said out loud defiantly.

"Anyone could want anything from her, Tiasa. Keep your thoughts to yourself," King Eurotas responded harshly.

"My apologies, Your Majesty," Tiasa replied emotionally.

King Eurotas said nothing. He sat there, dwindling with his thoughts that were running wild in his head. His crown carried the weight of the kingdom, and his heart carried the weight of worry for his daughter, the young princess.

A burst through the doors made Queen Clete jump, and she placed a hand over her chest to calm herself. Lacedaemon marched before King Eurotas with his guards at his side.

"King Eurotas," he said.

"Lacedaemon, I am at a loss for words and only extend my deepest apologies for what has befallen us and you," King

Eurotas replied, emotionally shook.

"There is no need for apologies, Your Majesty. I am just as upset as you are about what has happened."

"General Adamantios believes that someone inside the palace is responsible for Sparta's disappearance."

"Really? He is a man of logic and intelligence. I should like to think perhaps he is unfortunately right. However, I would like to request something of you, Your Majesty," Lacedaemon said stoically.

"What is your request, Lacedaemon?" King Eurotas asked.

"I should like your permission to find my betrothed. I should like to investigate this matter myself, and I mean no disrespect to General Adamantios, it's just, she is my wife. We were to marry today, and with what has befallen us, I would like to help where I can."

"We could use all of the help in the world. May the gods be with you and with us, and may they bring our Sparta home. Do what you will to find her," King Eurotas responded gratefully.

Lacedaemon bowed and walked back through the doors of the throne room, followed by his guards. They winded down the palace walls until they came to the openness of a terrace where vines flung out of flowerpots and pink flowers bloomed from them vibrantly.

"I overheard General Adamantios order a round-up of all the palace staff or those who have any reason to be within the walls," Basilius said to Lacedaemon.

Lacedaemon clicked his tongue and pursed his lips as he and his guards talked in confidant. "They couldn't have gotten far," Lacedaemon said.

"What if the young princess wasn't taken at all?" Callias asked boldly.

"That is quite the proposal, Callias," Kleon replied, questioning Callias's idea.

"He might be onto something, you know? Would a girl of her age willingly want to marry? No disrespect to you, Lacedaemon, as any woman would be lucky to receive your hand... but I wonder," Nicander chimed in intellectually.

"No offense taken, Nicander. Callias, you may be onto something. I understand this marriage has been arranged, and I am obliged to it, though I was not informed of Princess Sparta's age at the time of acceptance. A girl—nonetheless, a child—may fear marriage," Lacedaemon replied, thinking about that concept in his mind.

"Do you believe she's capable of running away?" Kleon asked.

"From what I have gathered, she has not been let out of the palace much, if at all. I imagine, because this is her home, she'd know how to break out of it better than anyone," Lacedaemon replied.

"So, she could have run away?" Basilius asked.

"Yes, she could have," Kleon answered for Lacedaemon.

"Then, where would she run to?" Callias asked.

"Anywhere, but somewhere," Lacedaemon replied.

Chapter IV

Lacedaemon, followed by his guards, marched into Princess Sparta's room. There was nothing out of place or out of order. In fact, the entire room looked immaculate. The rose-red curtains draped by the windows were tied neatly, and the bed hadn't even been slept in. The sheets remained unwrinkled, and the golden chalice by the bed still held water.

"It seems nothing is out of order... rather suspicious," Nicander said.

"Perhaps not. If she was not taken, then nothing should be out of order, which only means that she left willingly," Lacedaemon replied.

"Excuse me, Guard," Basilius called out to one of the guards down the hall.

"Yes. Is there something I may do for you?" the guard asked politely.

"Princess Sparta is guarded at night, is she not?"

"She is guarded every night. We even have patrols marching at all hours of the night to keep everyone safe."

"Thank you," Basilius said to the guard, who nodded his head in return.

"Timed patrols each and every night," Callias said to Basilius, overhearing the conversation between him and the guard.

"Yes, and that means the young princess would've known the timing of the patrol's rounds," Basilius replied.

"Lacedaemon, the patrols make rounds each and every night.

They are timed at all hours of the night, from what the guard has told me," Basilius said to Lacedaemon.

"Then, I have no doubt that the princess escaped," Lacedaemon replied.

"You're sure?" Kleon asked.

"Very much," Lacedaemon said.

"Where would she have gone?" Callias asked questioningly.

"I think I might have an idea," Nicander said quickly, staring out the window of Princess Sparta's room. Lacedaemon and his guards walked to the window Nicander was looking out of. Each of them stood, looking out at the view of the ocean, and in the distance, they could see the boats bobbing up and down on the dark blue waves. "If I wanted to escape here, I would go there," Nicander said, referring to the ocean and the boats.

"Let's go!" Lacedaemon said, as his guards followed him all the way out of the palace and through the city to the port of Laconia. The docks held boats, and many fishermen were offloading their catches of the day. Others were busy selling goods to the people of Laconia or to the visitors arriving at the port. The place was bustling and loud with noise.

Lacedaemon put a hand on his sword and walked around as his guards followed him like loyal hounds. "Excuse me," Lacedaemon said to a man.

"May I help you?" the man replied.

"I am wondering if anyone has seen a small girl with light brown hair and blue eyes running about?"

"I'm afraid not."

"Are you sure?" Lacedaemon said, showing the man his hand on his sword.

"I am sure, honest," the man said before continuing on. "Most people are busy buying goods and selling what catch they caught this morning. They're too occupied to have seen anything," the man replied truthfully.

"Thank you for your time. Our apologies for bothering you," Lacedaemon replied.

"You're welcome. Are you guards for the palace?" the man asked curiously.

"If we were?" Kleon interjected suggestively.

"A boat is missing; maybe the girl you're after has taken it. We haven't been able to find it, but if you do find it, please return it to us. We are in great need of it," the man said before walking away with a crate of crabs in his arms.

"Even if she did take the boat, where would she go?" Basilius asked questioningly.

"You're right. A girl of such a young age rowing out into the ocean. It'd be risky," Lacedaemon said.

"She had to do it at night," Nicander chimed in.

"It would explain how she wouldn't have been seen by anyone here," Kleon said.

"Where would she even go?" Callias said, before saying, "The only thing close to here is the island of Cythera."

"That has an even bigger port and is known as a frequent stopping point for many who sail the Aegean Sea," Lacedaemon responded, thinking quickly before saying, "She's trying to flee farther away. Nicander, go inform King Eurotas of our discovery and run as quickly as you can back here. Basilius, prepare all the ships and all the guards to be ready to leave the instant Nicander gets back."

"All ships and all guards?" Basilius asked Lacedaemon, a bit shocked at the order.

"Yes. We don't know who we will encounter or what we will be up against when going to retrieve her. Quickly, we don't know how far ahead of us she is," Lacedaemon responded with rushed authority.

Nicander ran with great speed and informed King Eurotas and Queen Clete of Lacedaemon's theory. While King Eurotas was unsure whose theory to believe—Lacedaemon or General Adamantios—he knew that one of them had to be right. He ordered additional ships and guards to follow Lacedaemon's command in order to bring his daughter back.

Nicander arrived back at the port swiftly, and the additional guards boarded, as all prepared to sail for the island of Cythera. The red sails of the ships blew in the wind as the breeze pushed them forward through the rippled waves. Lacedaemon stood on the bow, keeping his eyes peeled for any sign of Sparta or the island. He hoped that he would find her, but a part of him also hoped he would not.

To be wed to a child was an insult to him, or perhaps he should be flattered that she was a king's daughter. Lacedaemon would honor his promise of trying to find Sparta, but if he came up empty-handed, he knew that King Eurotas would stop at nothing until she was found. This only meant that his feelings were in more turmoil than ever, and in many ways, he was angry. He fought alongside King Eurotas, who in turn offered his child daughter to him—Lacedaemon, a son of Zeus—all while neglecting to tell him of her age.

It was intentionally left out; Lacedaemon knew that. However, he wondered how he could possibly change his fate or if it could be changed at all?

Chapter V

Island of Cythera

The young boy grabbed the tangerine and peeled it calmly. I could tell that he was hungry, and once he reached the fruit inside, he ate it quickly. "Thank you," he said.

"You're most welcome. What is your name?" I asked him politely.

"Sophus," he replied before asking, "What is yours?"

"Zosime," I replied, knowing I could never give him my real name. If anyone found out that I was Sparta, princess of Laconia, I could end up in danger, or someone may even bring me back to the palace in exchange for reward. I would have to be careful about my identity and what I told people who asked questions about me.

Sophus smiled at me before getting back to work. He brought the man who offered me passage the barrels of fish. The man began gutting the fish, and Sophus sat there, helping him. I began walking around the port and stopped in front of a woman who sat on a crate behind her table. She had lots of jewelry displayed, and they were the most intricate of designs. Many had colored beads, beautiful rocks, pieces of bone, and some were even made of silver and gold. I stood there, admiring her talent.

"Excuse me," a voice said from behind. I turned my head and saw one of the fishermen speaking with the guards, guards who had a Laconian emblem. I panicked and tripped over my feet, trying to run. My trip had been heard by the guards, and a man I did not recognize turned his head. I didn't stop to stare or look at him as I ran away as fast as I could. My breath was fueled with anxiety, but I pushed on, and ran faster through the crowds of people and through the market on the port.

I could hear the footsteps chasing after me, and I knew the guards had been rigorously trained for battle, meaning they knew how to run. I knew they would have no trouble catching up to me, and I could hear them yelling, "Stop!" but I did not stop; I kept running. If I could make it to the jungle, I knew I had a chance of escaping them. I could hide and maybe they wouldn't find me, but now that they knew I was here, they would search the whole island until they found me.

"This way!" a voice said to my side before grabbing my arm. I followed Sophus as we pushed past the people and winded in between market vendors. "Everyone, step aside!" I heard someone yell, and the people did exactly that. The guards now had a clear path to where I was and began running swiftly after me.

Sophus turned a sharp corner, and my cloak snagged on a nail, sticking out of the dock. It ripped off my chest, but I didn't have time to unhook it or get it back. I had to keep running, and I followed Sophus on his heels as I hoped he'd have a way out of this labyrinth of a port. He veered around another corner, and I saw a stone wall. "Up here!" he said, as we both scaled the stone wall and jumped over it, only to begin running again.

"Through here," he said as I followed him through a grove of trees and to the beach, where a small boat lay docked. "Hurry! Push it into the water," Sophus was panicking. We both heaved our strength and pushed the small boat into the water and jumped into it. I grabbed one oar, and he grabbed the other, as we both began frantically rowing.

"Lacedaemon! Over here!" a voice shouted. The man I was

betrothed to was here. He was here searching for me, trying to find me, to bring me back to Laconia to marry him. *That will never happen,* I thought to myself, and rowed my own oar harder. Sophus rowed too, and together we made it out to sea. We steered away from the port and around a massive cliff that had waves smashing against it.

Once around it, we were hidden from view. I could see a ship anchored in the distance and knew that was where we were headed to.

"Keep rowing. We're almost there!" Sophus said to me, and I nodded in acknowledgement. The wind blew harshly, and the waves seemed to turn into sweltering masses that threatened to tip our boat. I felt nauseated but didn't stop rowing.

We made it to the ship, and a skinny man in a white shirt grabbed Sophus's arm and yanked him up. He grabbed my arm and yanked me up next. I fell onto the dock of the boat and looked at Sophus who was panting heavily like me. We were both relieved to be on board. "You weren't supposed to be back yet," the skinny man said.

"Change of plans," Sophus replied before saying, "Theron wants us to go out for another haul. The port is busy today."

"If he says so," the man replied, and with that, the sails hoisted and the ship began sailing around the island. I lost view of the cliff as we headed out into the depths of the deep blue sea. The crew was busy untangling nets and traps for fish, crabs, or whatever else they could catch.

Sophus looked at me as we sat together side by side near the crate barrels on the ship.

"Who is she, exactly?" a man with four fingers inquired.

"She's new help," Sophus replied.

The man didn't question Sophus, and we both quickly rose

to our feet. "Hold the rope, and I'll begin tying it," Sophus said to me. I did what he said and held the rope, so he could begin tying it. "Who are you, really?" he whispered to me. I felt I could no longer lie, as his act of bravery could get him killed if he were to be caught.

"I am Princess Sparta of Laconia," I replied back, whispering in his ear.

Sophus looked at me, puzzled before saying, "What are you doing here, and why were you running away from the guards?"

"I am arranged to be married today and then taken someplace far away. I don't want to be married to a man I've never met and so I decided to run away," I responded quietly.

"You're running away?"

"Yes."

"Where will you go now?" he asked me, still fiddling with the ropes.

"As far away from here as possible," I replied.

"I won't tell anyone who you are, but do as I say, and I'll make sure you get as far away from here as possible," Sophus said to me with a small smile.

"Thank you," I said, smiling in return.

Sophus turned to the skinny man and said, "How much would it cost for you to sail this boat to Ithaca?"

"Are you asking me to ditch Theron? Boy, that is dangerous and stupid," the skinny man replied.

"How much?" Sophus said again.

"Too much," he replied.

"Would this cover it?" Sophus asked, holding up a gold cuff that was bejeweled. I realized it was mine, and he had swiped it off my wrist when I wasn't looking.

"Where'd you get this?" the skinny man asked, looking at

the gold-bejeweled cuff.

"Swiped it off a table. Do we have a deal?"

"All right. We sail to Ithaca!" the skinny man said as the crew began rushing around, busily organizing things on the deck and tending to the ship.

I smiled at Sophus as a "thank you," and I watched the sails turn as one crewman veered around the mast, spinning the sails with him. The wind caught the massive cotton-white sheets with ease, and we began being pulled in another direction, out into the Aegean Sea. I watched as the ship bounced up and down through the waves, sometimes breaking through them.

I looked up and saw the light blue sky had milky cream-colored clouds rolling among its vastness. I could see seagulls squawking from above and circling around our ship in bouts. The skinny man looked at the horizon and stood behind the wheel, looking like a true captain of courage. I could tell, even though he was not the captain or the owner of this vessel, he had all of the experience necessary to pilot it. A man of true talent, and one who could be an explorer if he wanted.

I stood at the bow, feeling the wind ripple through my hair and dress as it guided us on our journey to Ithaca. I had seen maps of Ithaca and knew that it would take us a long while to get there. Still, I remained thankful for all that had happened today, and I smiled happily.

Chapter VI

Voyage to Ithaca

The ship rocked against the Mediterranean waves that seemed higher than those of the Aegean Sea. We would rise upward and fall downward quickly; it made my stomach feel queasy, and many times, I felt I would be sick. Sophus had explained to me that the rough seas could indicate a coming storm.

"You have to pay attention to the sea. It'll tell you what's coming ahead," the skinny man said to me. I had come to know him as "captain" or by his real name, Philo. He turned to me and said, "The waves grow higher, and the wind blows harder. The skies seem clear now, but a storm is coming."

"A storm?" I replied, worried.

"Don't worry. We will make it through," he responded to me reassuringly. I had faith in him, but I wasn't sure how much. If the storm was going to be as rough as the seas are now, then I had every right to be concerned. I watched as the ship dipped forward and then heaved back up again. Philo was a great captain and piloted the ship with ease. He was used to the choppy seas; but I was not and battled the nausea building in my throat.

"The more you get used to ship life, the easier it is to deal with the sea sickness," Sophus said to me, putting a hand on my shoulder. I smiled at him in thanks for his comfort and care.

Over the past week, Sophus had taught me much about life at sea. I had learned how to tie knots and what each one was used for. Some of the crewmen even taught me what net was used to catch what, and I even learned how to fish. Philo taught me how to use a knife to carefully gut a fish. He showed me how to cut the meat finely off of the bones, and I was beginning to enjoy life out on the water.

I had been locked away in the palace for so long that I never knew the feeling of true freedom; and this was it. I was surrounded by a never-ending sea of blue, and it made me feel alive. I was able to do things I would never have been allowed to do in the palace, and there was a feeling of boldness to finally being able to do things myself for once.

It was when I snapped out of my thoughts that I saw the dark thunderous clouds creeping in the distance. I could see the lightning dance across the sky in sharp, thin bolts. The sea began growing restless and rocked the ship even more. I grabbed the railing to steady myself for fear of falling overboard. Sophus grabbed a railing next to me, and together we held on, bracing ourselves for the storm.

The rain began pelting down in what felt like hail. I could hardly see anything around me, and the mist from the sea swatted my face as if threatening to pull me overboard. I held on tighter as my hair stuck to my face and the back of my neck. I could hear the crewmen shouting at each other, and I heard Philo's voice from behind. The wind blew his words away from me, and all I caught was a noise I couldn't understand.

The clouds were a dark gray-ashen color, and the thunder beat like drums from above. It pounded in my ears and through my body as if somebody were using a mallet to pound the sound down from the heavens. The lightning shot down from the sky and struck the water around us in a fury. I could see the flashes through the booms, and it made the whole escapade all the more overwhelming.

I felt my feet sliding on the deck, and I struggled to hang

onto the side of the ship. Sophus was wrapped so tight around the railing, clinging to it for dear life. The ship jolted upward and slammed back down into the sea. I shot upward and felt myself collide with the ship's dock as I was forced back onto it. My body hit hard, and everything within me turned into a sharp pain. I didn't have time to cope or deal with the pains; I had to hang onto something, anything, before we hit another wave.

    I grabbed onto some rope and tied myself to the ship's railing as securely as I could. I touched my head to feel the warmth of blood coating my fingertips. The rain came down even harder as it fell from the skies, and I could hear what sounded like screams echoing in the distance that were carried to my ears by the wind.

    I heard the thunder again and saw the lightning jolt across the sky as if chasing something in the dark clouds above. I saw the crewmen clinging to barrels and rope, trying to steady themselves for the next oncoming wave. The water crashed onto the deck, and objects began rolling in every which way.

    The ship tilted upward and then sped down the steep wave at an incline. I heard screams and what sounded like something cracking. I braced myself as the noise grew louder.

Chapter VII

The salt water burned my lungs and stung my eyes. I felt the coldness of the sea around me, and I hung onto a barrel as I struggled to keep conscious. My head throbbed, and I could feel the pain ringing through my head, like a bell being continuously chimed. The waves pulled me over and under, viciously threatening to drown me. I held my breath and braced myself as I was dragged farther down into the sea. I arose quickly to the surface and clung to the barrel, still bobbing over the waves.

The storm was still raging, and I could tell the ship had been broken into pieces by the amount of material floating around me. The white sails floated on the surface of the rolling waves as the rain continued to pour down from above. The lightning flashed, and I could see boxes, crates, and parts of the ship's mast beginning to sink. The thunder crashed through the clouds and startled me. I almost lost grip of the barrel but knew that if I let go, I would sink to the depths of the ocean, just like the remnants of our ship.

I coughed and gasped for air as another wave threw me across the sea. I was being thrown around, wave after wave, as each pulled me in another direction. I tried to get my bearings to see if there was something else I could grab onto or perhaps swim to land, but I could see nothing in the haze of the storm. The salt water spurted upward, and I was thrust under, losing grip of the barrel.

I struggled to reach the surface of the sea, but another wave pushed me down even farther into the deep blue ocean, and I knew there was no fighting against it. I took my last breath, and I had sacrificed everything for my freedom. This was it. I closed my eyes and let the ocean pull me into the dark depths below.

*

I could hear the sound of waves crashing in my ears and felt a throbbing sensation in the back of my head. I lifted my head and opened my eyes to be blinded by bright light. I looked down to see golden-colored sand beneath me. I slowly turned my head to see that I had somehow made it to land. The waves crashed against rocks, and the evergreen trees swayed in the wind. It was as if the storm never happened at all.

I slowly rose to sit on my knees and pulled my hair, which was stuck to my face, away from my eyes to see more clearly. My dress was ripped at the shoulder, and blood oozed out of the cut on my arm. I placed my fingers on the wound on my head and felt the tenderness of pain and warm blood. I turned around slowly to stare out into the ocean.

There were many pieces of wood that the waves had placed on the beach. I saw some barrels and crates that were making their way toward me as they rode the tide in. I could see rope flung onto the rocks, and pieces of the sails lay snagged on a fallen tree. I did not see anyone, and I squinted my eyes further to get a better look into the distance, but saw no one in sight. I was the only survivor.

I stood up and climbed slowly onto one of the tall rocks, then once again peered out into the distance. I still saw no one, but I hoped that maybe I would get a glimpse of Sophus. I prayed that he or Philo somehow survived the vicious storm, but I saw nothing, and I knew my prayers would not be answered. They were both at the bottom of the Mediterranean Sea and were now in the realm above.

Tears slid down my cheeks, and I let out my sobs. "You've been through much, child?" a voice said next to me. I looked over to see a beautiful woman looking up at me. She sat perched on a rock, and a closer glance at her made me realize that she was a siren. The half-human, half-fish looked at me with sparkly blue eyes, and her blonde hair flowed down at the sides of her face neatly.

"Did you cause this?" I asked her, pointing to the shipwreck and death that had befallen me.

"No. The storm did," she replied calmly.

"You saved me?" I asked.

"*We* did," she said to me, and I saw more sirens rising from the sea.

"Why?" I questioned, confused.

"You are no sailor."

"You could've saved the rest of them," I said, letting more tears fall from my eyes.

"We were not supposed to," she responded quietly.

"But why?"

"We were only told to save you."

"Who told you to save me?" I asked emotionally.

"I am not allowed to tell," the siren said, staring at me curiously.

I was frustrated and said, "I get to live, but everyone else has to die?"

"We don't help sailors, but you are no sailor. We were asked to swim into the storm and find you. In exchange, we keep your shiny treasure," the siren said, referring to my gold-bejeweled cuff lying around her wrist.

I breathed in, knowing that I wasn't going to get the answers I wanted from her, and said, "Thank you."

"We were also told to protect you and help you survive here," she said with a small smile.

"I just want to go home," I replied, defeated.

"I'm afraid you are not supposed to go home."

"What do you mean? There has to be a way for me to get home?"

"You are to stay here until we are told to let you leave," she replied cunningly.

"Someone has commanded you to keep me here. Why?" I asked angrily.

"We don't know. We just do what has been asked of us."

"How long must I stay?"

"Until we are told to let you leave."

"If I try to leave before I am allowed to leave?" I asked with red eyes questioningly.

"We'll drown you," she responded coldly.

Chapter VIII

Island of Cythera

Basilius clutched the cloak belonging to Princess Sparta in his hands. Lacedaemon and his guards ran over quickly and stopped.

"It's hers," Kleon said.

"We were right. She's here," Lacedaemon responded, looking around at his surroundings.

"She couldn't have gotten far," Callias said.

"Search all the buildings and leave nothing unturned. Kleon, inform the rest of the guards that she is on the island, and to begin searching everything and everyone at once. She is here, hiding somewhere, and we *will* find her. Basilius, go to Laconia and inform King Eurotas of our findings. Take the cloak as proof that she is here," Lacedaemon said with authority. His guards did exactly as he said, and every building was being upheaved and searched for Princess Sparta of Laconia.

Where could she have gone?" Lacedaemon thought to himself, *We were right behind her*, he thought again before looking at the stone wall before him. "Nicander!" he shouted.

"Yes?" Nicander replied.

"We're going over the wall," Lacedaemon replied, as he and Nicander scaled the stone wall with ease. Together, they marched down onto the beach and stared out into the sea. They both saw nothing, but Nicander walked over to a rock that seemed out of place.

"Lacedaemon," he said, as Lacedaemon walked over to stand next to him.

"There are footprints and marks in the sand which indicate that a boat was beached here. It looks as if someone helped her push the boat out into the ocean. The rock was the anchor, and here's the rope," Nicander said, holding the rope in his hands.

"They cannot be far, and it'll be easier to see them in the ocean. We'll climb that cliff and see if we can spot them, then give the order to sail in pursuit of them. I want to be sure they are in the water and didn't sail around the cliff, trying to make us think that they are out to sea, when *really*, they are still here on the island," Lacedaemon responded strategically.

"Lead the way," Nicander said as he followed Lacedaemon. Together, the two men braved the steep, jagged cliff and climbed carefully up to the top. The breeze blew the hair out of Lacedaemon's eyes as he stood up, right on top of the cliff. Nicander stood next to him, panting and wiping the sweat off his forehead.

"There," Nicander said, pointing to a ship in the distance. Lacedaemon and Nicander could see a man wearing a white shirt pulling up a small boy and young girl from a row boat.

"They're going to help her escape," Lacedaemon said, panicking.

"Then we must stop them," Nicander replied as he and Lacedaemon quickly scaled down the jagged cliff. Lacedaemon nicked his shoulder on the way down, and a small stream of blood began to slide down his arm. Though, he did not care. The two men ran with great propriety and scaled the stone wall to rush back to the port.

"They're trying to flee. Quickly, draw the sails and begin rowing!" Lacedaemon yelled. The guards quickly followed his orders and took their place as the ships began traveling through the waves in pursuit of Princess Sparta.

The vast ships were long in length, and their dark red sails caught the wind with such strength that the men rowing could stop wasting their energy. The wind carried the ships around the jagged cliff that Lacedaemon and Nicander had scaled. Lacedaemon stood there clutching the bow of the ship with his hands, eager to try to find the ship that had taken away his betrothed. He saw nothing.

"If we keep up our pace, we should spot them in no time," Nicander said to Lacedaemon, looking out in the distance. Lacedaemon nodded his head and kept his eyes peeled for the ship. He knew that they couldn't have gotten far, and that his ships were far mightier and faster than the one Princess Sparta was sailing in.

Lacedaemon breathed in and kept up his confidence, despite his feelings about the situation. He knew that by the end of the day, he would have the young girl aboard his ship, and together, they would be sailing back to Laconia and get married instantly. How he wished he hadn't been so hasty to accept King Eurotas's offer, and how he imagined escaping a choice that wasn't his. He felt everything was beyond his control and even considered praying to his father.

However, he knew deep down that his prayers and wishes would not be answered. Nor would anyone come to save him from such a choice that he felt was a mistake. His heart ached for a way out, but he knew that there wasn't one. He would marry the young princess, and live with his decision and feelings of regret for the rest of his life.

The sea breeze picked up and sprayed mist into Lacedaemon's face, which broke him from his thoughts. He looked up at the clouds and saw the once white cotton balls were now turning a dark gray. A storm was approaching, and they were sailing straight for it.

Chapter IX

"Fall back!" Lacedaemon shouted to all of his guards and the rest of the ships.

"If we retreat, we'll lose her," Nicander said to Lacedaemon.

"If we don't retreat now, we will all be lost. Fall back!" Lacedaemon replied and screamed. The ships began turning their sails and everyone frantically tried to change direction before the clouds overcame them. The sails swiftly caught the wind and pushed the ships back toward the island and port of Cythera.

The clouds creeped toward the ships, almost chasing them. Lacedaemon was sure the storm was a sign that he was not supposed to pursue the young princess, but a part of him also wondered if perhaps his father had heard his prayers and had sent a storm to kill the young girl. He did not wish for her to die; he only wished he did not have to marry her, but the only way he would be freed of his obligation would be if she were to die.

Lacedaemon felt guilty, as if he were being saved and punished at the same time. He heard the thunder from above and felt it shake through his core. The lightning danced in the distance, and he could see the flashes of it amongst the dark clouds. He glanced back to see the crashing of the rain against the waves, and he could see the swells that grew more immense with each passing second.

He knew deep down that there was no way anyone was going to make it out of that storm. A "sailor's doom" is what many referred to it as—a sudden storm that was meant to sink and destroy any ship that entered its fury. It would leave no survivors and decimate everything in its path. There was nothing he could do but watch from his ship as the storm grew in density. He could hear the rain pelting off of the seas, and he could see the waves thrashing vigorously.

Nicander walked over and placed a hand on Lacedaemon's shoulder. "We'll search the waters tomorrow for survivors," Nicander said, hopeful. Lacedaemon nodded his head, but deep down knew that Nicander's offer of hope was one out of sorrow. For he, too, knew that no one survived a "sailor's doom" and tomorrow, they would be looking for the young girl's body to bring home to Laconia.

The ships reached the port and the people were frantically packing up all of their belongings as if knowing that the storm was coming. The guards worked quickly to dock the ships and tie them securely. Nicander and Lacedaemon walked briskly toward a building where a kind woman had welcomed him and his guards. They bunkered down and waited for what was yet to come.

The woman offered plates of bread, cheese, and fish. She offered drinks of ale and told stories that were passed onto her from when she was a child. Lacedaemon and his guards listened intently.

"Everyone knows the stories of the gods and the Titans, but my mother spoke of a story of the ancients. A story about us, humans. In the days where land remained unnamed and oceans had yet to be sailed. The days where the sun and the moon rose and fell together. These were the days before we discovered the gods and the Titans. There were forests with trees as tall as the eye can see, and lakes as deep as the mountains. Beasts lurked in the woods and hunted wherever they pleased, and we had to learn to live with the dangers that roamed around us.

One day, when the crescent moon glowed from above, a beast with wild claws and golden eyes came from the depths of the forest and slaughtered many. A man rose up and chose to take a hunting party to kill the beast that had attacked them. They tracked it for days, and when they finally found it, no one survived, except one. The man who had led the expedition came back with only one arm and told the tale of the monster that had attacked and killed the rest of the hunters.

As the days went on, more grew concerned about the beast's return. It was decided that once again, the now one-armed man would lead a party of stronger hunters to the beast's den. They had more men this time, and together, they marched through the forest and toward the ferocity that awaited them. Once again, the one-armed man returned a day later. He told another tale of how none of the men survived and he had to run for his life. The people were beside themselves with grief and worry; after all, if no one could slay the beast, then how would they all be safe?

The people worked together to make weapons with sharper blades and pointier tips. They worked tirelessly into the nights and throughout the day to make swords and axes that could slice a man in half with just one strike. They fashioned spears with longer and sharper arrowed tips.

This time, they sent the one-armed man with a battalion of men into the forest with these new weapons. The men were confident they would slay the beast this time, but once again, only the one-armed man returned. He told the people how the beast was made of armor and that their weapons couldn't penetrate such a monster.

The people were angry that the beast had slaughtered so many, and they decided that tomorrow—together—they would all march out and slay the dreaded beast. An army would be no match for such a predator, and when the sun awoke in the morning, the people armed themselves and went into the forest. Some were scared, and some were angry. Some were ready to kill the beast, and some were ready to run for their lives.

When they reached the beast's den, they saw the bones of their comrades and the great, strong men they had sent into battle. The sharp and cunning weapons lay broken on the ground in fragments. A low growl could be heard from inside the cave, and the army readied themselves for battle. The beast lunged out of its den and let out a wild scream. It swallowed the whole army but left the one-armed man alive to return to tell of what had become of the army.

He returned again, and the women were havocked with worry. It was decided that they would call on other tribes to come help them slay the beast, and perhaps they would have weapons or greater manpower to slay it. When the sun set, a young girl who had been eagerly listening to the tales the one-armed man had told and who had seen the destruction the beast had caused, decided to venture into the forest herself.

She followed the path that could be seen easily, as the men had frequented it enough times for it to be visible. The young girl trekked down the path, and when she reached the beast's den, she saw the bones and skulls of men lying on the ground, along with the weapons that were scattered everywhere. She even saw the shadows of where the army had stood, ready to battle the deadly monster.

A low growl came from inside the cave, but the fearless girl walked right in. She stumbled over bones and had a hard time seeing in the darkness, but when she felt the heat breathing on her from the beast's nostrils, she wasn't the least bit frightened. The beast opened its golden eyes that burned in a rage, yet he did not attack the girl. He stared at her, and the girl walked up to it, placing her hand on the beast's head. She gave it a kiss, and the beast embraced the girl's empathy.

"Why must everyone try to harm you when you are just as hungry as we are? We hunt all of the food you eat and leave none for you. You are hungry and need to eat too," the young girl said as she stroked the beast's head. The beast seemed to understand the girl and welcomed her kindness and understanding.

The next day, the girl strolled into the camp with the mighty beast at her side. The people panicked and began gathering their weapons, but the beast did not attack; he stood at the girl's side, staring at the people before him. The young girl smiled and petted the beast on the head.

"Get away from it before it kills you!" the one-armed man screamed. "It will not harm me or any of us. We must share food with it, and it will leave us alone," she said. The one-armed man laughed, and the beast opened its large jaws showing its jagged teeth, and ate the man. The people agreed to listen to the girl out of fear, and they began sharing food with the beast, and in turn, the beast left them alone.

"That's quite the story," Lacedaemon said to the woman.

"I reckon we would have no trouble slaying such a beast," Nicander said as the guards and Lacedaemon began laughing.

"You did not listen to the story," the woman remarked.

"We did listen, and they were clearly underprepared and had no plan of attack," Lacedaemon replied.

"The story is not about battle," the woman said a bit bitterly.

"Then what was it about?" Nicander asked boastfully.

"Why you should never send men to do a woman's job," she replied with a sleek smile.

"Fair point," Lacedaemon remarked, sipping his cup of ale.

The guards and Nicander smiled at the lesson of the story and began hearing thunder in the distance. They could feel the ground begin to shake and saw flashes of lightning from above.

Nicander looked out the window to see the wind blowing mist off the waves, and he could see the ocean roaring with anger. The guards stiffened as another loud boom of thunder sounded from above and reverberated through them. Lacedaemon could see the dark clouds rolling over them, and he felt—in some way—he was being punished. He even felt a bit frightened at the loudness of the storm that roared from the heavens.

Lacedaemon was no stranger to battle, and he heard the screams and cries of his enemies before he slaughtered them. He had heard the pounding of shields and stampede of footsteps, yet he never wavered. The son of Zeus stood his ground; he held his sword and fought with valiance, but this storm made him uneasy. He thought of the young princess, and in some weird way, his heart began to yearn for her, or maybe he was preparing himself for the guilt he would feel if he found her floating lifeless amongst the waves. He took another sip of ale and tried to numb his feelings, but found no drink which would stop the feelings of remorse that had fully submerged him in regret.

Chapter X

The Beach

Sparta looked out into the distance as she sat on the sand and stared at the stars. They shined brightly and twinkled in the midnight-colored sky. The ocean was calm as the waves rolled in and out. A light breeze blew her hair from her eyes, and she stared back down at the small fire she had started.

The sirens kept their word and had helped her survive. They told her how to use sticks and the art of friction to create an ember that would turn into flame. The blonde siren, whose name she had come to learn as Nerissa, had told her of plants that held healing sap that she applied to wounds on her head and shoulder.

Nerissa caught fish from the ocean and brought them to Sparta, who used a sharp rock she had found to gut the fish like Philo had taught her. She speared the meat of the fish with sticks and placed them over the fire to cook. The meat darkened and tendered quickly. The feeling of hunger had set in, and Sparta began eating the juicy, cooked meat happily.

She had found that drinking water from coconuts was more sustainable than searching for a water source. The storm had knocked the near life out of her, and with the little energy she had, she felt she shouldn't waste it. It was only her first night of how many; she did not know.

In fact, Sparta wasn't even sure where she was. Was she off the coast of Laconia, or was she closer to Pylos? Perhaps neither, or maybe she was on an island. The sirens did say they would drown her if she tried to leave, but what if she could escape by venturing deeper into the jungle that surrounded her?

Sparta decided it was not a good idea. She didn't know what lay in the jungle and thought it was best not to anger the gods again. The sudden storm had killed the people she had come to know as friends. They had risked their lives to help her escape her fate, and in turn, had died for it. She should have died too, but was somehow spared from the wrath of the storm. It only made sense that the gods had intervened, and this was her punishment for trying to escape marriage to Lacedaemon.

The sirens swam in the distance, and Sparta could see their finned tails surfacing amongst the waves before they dove under again. She wrapped herself tightly in her dress that was torn and still damp, as she tried to comfort herself. The sand provided a pillow for her head, and she laid down exhausted from what the day had brought her.

Sparta closed her eyes and let her thoughts drift away until she could no longer see them. The darkness slipped over her, and she fell into a deep slumber. The sirens bounced through the waves, and Nerissa emerged to see Sparta curled up by the fire, asleep. She knew it was not like her kind to help humans, but when it was asked of her by the gods or a god, they were to obey. In many ways, her short time with the young princess had made her protective, and she even sympathized with her situation.

Nerissa dove back under the waves and joined her sisters to begin hunting. The stars shimmered amongst the waves as the sirens swam in the dark waters that clouded visibility. They clicked and chirped at one another—like dolphins would—to communicate to each other. Their long tails propelled them through the cold sea with ease and everything was calm.

*

The sun rose the next morning, and its light shone into Sparta's eyes. She woke up with a yawn and wiped the sand off her cheek. Her head still pulsed, and the pain in her shoulder hurt with a sharpness. The sun's rays gleamed along the surface of the ocean, and Sparta saw the sirens' tails sparkling through the waves as the light reflected off their shimmering scales.

The sky was clear and cheery blue. The clouds rolled through the sky in strides, and the wind blew salty air through her hair. Sparta gazed out at the distance and looked at her surroundings. She had accepted her predicament as a punishment and would remain here forever, if that was what the gods wished.

Sparta stood and looked back out at the sea. She squinted her eyes sharply and saw deep red sails in the distance. Her eyes widened, and she quickly began waving her arms and screaming, "Help!" "Over here!" "Help!" Sparta screamed and ran for the rocks, trying to allow the ships to see her and come to her rescue. She stood on the rocks, screaming and waving her arms.

Nerissa rose to the surface of the water and heard the screams of Sparta. She knew those ships in the distance were searching for the young princess, and knew she could not let her be found. The other sirens surfaced, and they too, saw the ships with big red sails in the distance. Nerissa hissed at her sisters, and they left quickly.

Sparta still screamed and screamed until her voice began to crack. Nerissa climbed the rock and grabbed Sparta's feet, causing them both to fall into the ocean. Sparta struggled to surface, but Nerissa helped her and held her slimy hand over the mouth of the young girl to silence her hope-filled screams.

"You must be quiet!" Nerissa said to Sparta.

"They are looking for me," Sparta replied.

"Yes, they are, but you are to remain here," Nerissa said as she began to hear Sparta sob. The waves flowed past them, and even though Nerissa could not see Sparta's tears, she knew the girl was crying. A part of her felt bad for what she had to do but knew it needed to be done. The young princess was to stay here as long as Poseidon commanded it.

For the great god of the seas had heard the commotion upstairs from his brother Zeus and decided to intervene before the girl insulted his son, Lacedaemon, any further. Sparta was to remain here for as long as he willed it, and in many ways, it seemed like a punishment but Poseidon knew it was a blessing.

The sea nymphs and deities of prophecy had told him so. There was a reason for everything, and sometimes, intervening was necessary to ensure that what must happen in the future was back on track. It was only when he was certain that things were going as they should, he would release the girl.

Chapter XI

Port of Cythera

Lacedaemon and his crew woke up early. They quickly prepared the ships for take-off and assessed the storm damage. The wind had blown tree branches and leaves into the port, but it was nothing that couldn't be moved easily. The guards were hasty to board the ships, and at Lacedaemon's command, they set sail for where they last saw Sparta on the fleeing ship.

The sea was calm and peaceful, as if the storm had never happened at all. Kleon stood at the bow of the ship with Lacedaemon, keeping their eyes peeled for the ship they knew had been ripped apart by the "sailor's doom." The horizon was glistening, and the light from the sun gleamed off of the water, which helped everyone to see if there was any wreckage floating about.

"There!" Nicander yelled, and all eyes turned toward barrels and rope bobbing in the waves. Lacedaemon and his crew hoisted the remnants found in the water onto their ship. As they sailed further into the path where the storm had been, more and more pieces of the ship wreck could be seen roaming the sea.

Lacedaemon kept his eyes peeled and attentive as he searched the waters for the young princess.

"Over here!" a guard shouted, and Lacedaemon watched Basilius and Callias pull a lifeless body from the sea. It was the man in the white shirt who had been seen helping Sparta and the young boy climb aboard the day before. The guards stood and looked at the dead man aboard their ship and thoughtfully placed a wool blanket over his body in solace and respect.

The ships sailed on after a small prayer was said for the man in the white shirt. The wind lifted the red sails, and they flew through the ocean with great power. Lacedaemon could see more parts of the ship floating in the sea, and he knew eventually they would find Sparta drifting amongst the remnants.

He breathed a great breath in and prepared himself for what was yet to come. The guards had pulled another lifeless body out of the ocean, and it was an older gentleman with four fingers on one hand. There was still no sign of the young princess, and Lacedaemon was growing anxious. His anxiety and anticipation rose every minute that they did not find her.

King Eurotas was not aware of the storm but only that his daughter was somewhere on the island. Now, Lacedaemon would have to tell the great king of her death, and the entire Kingdom of Laconia would be in tears. His thoughts kept interrupting his focus, and his heart beat with trepidation as the ships pounded through the oncoming waves.

The wind blew fiercely in his face, but Lacedaemon remained steadfast, keeping his gaze on the water. "Help!" a voice echoed through the wind. Lacedaemon turned his head but saw nothing. He turned his eyes toward the land and squinted, searching for who was calling for his help. "Help me!" The voice echoed again.

"Did you hear that?" Lacedaemon asked Kleon.

"I did. There must be someone in the water," Kleon replied.

Lacedaemon and Kleon frantically searched the water with their eyes and moved around the ship, trying to locate who was calling for their aid. The wind kept blowing, and the two kept their ears sharp, listening again for the voice that sounded desperate. They heard nothing.

Kleon looked toward the far away land they were sailing past and could see rocks on a flat of sand with a thicket of jungle in the background. He did not see anyone calling or shouting for help, even though he had heard it. Lacedaemon looked too, but he saw nothing.

"I suppose our minds are playing tricks on us," Lacedaemon said to Kleon in disappointment.

"It seems you are right. We've been searching for hours in the heat of the sun... we must be hearing things," Kleon replied.

The ships sailed past the land and continued on, still searching the waters for the young princess or anyone who may have survived the treacherous storm. The waves flowed smoothly, and the light blue waters created great visibility. All was calm as the guards kept their focus sharp.

A small "bang" jolted the ship, and Lacedaemon hung onto the bow for support.

"We must've hit something," he said, walking toward the back of the ship. The guards began heaving up a big part of the mast with some sail still attached to it. They placed it carefully onto the deck, and Kleon stared at it intently. He began unwrapping the bunched-up part of the sail and turned to Lacedaemon with sorrowful eyes.

"I don't believe we'll find the young princess because it appears that she went down with the ship," Kleon said, holding up Sparta's golden bejeweled cuff. Lacedaemon breathed in tearfully and said, "We are done searching! She has gone down with the ship, and this is proof that she has left this world. A moment of silence and a prayer for our loss."

The guards obeyed and all bowed their heads in solace for the death of Princess Sparta of Laconia. Lacedaemon did not think he would be so emotional; after all, he didn't want to marry the young girl anyway, but the thought of her death made his eyes wet, and he wasn't sure why. Perhaps it was the death of a girl so young, or maybe it was because he felt guilty in conscious that he may have caused a part in her death.

"We will sail to Laconia," Lacedaemon declared, and the ships turned around at once to begin the journey back to the kingdom to inform all of the tragic news. Basilius placed a hand on Lacedaemon's shoulder, and together, they stood staring out at the vastness of the great ocean.

*

Their arrival to the Kingdom of Laconia was much anticipated. The palace was booming with excitement at news of Princess Sparta's return. Lacedaemon reluctantly told King Eurotas and Queen Clete of his endeavors to not only track down the young girl but to recover her from the ocean.

Tiasa sobbed and wept as Queen Clete tried to conceal her sadness but could not stop the tears from pouring down her face. She excused herself and left the throne room in a haste. Her maids followed, but she ran to her quarters and shut the door quickly behind herself. She dropped to the floor and let out a scream that ripped through the palace with such vigor that everyone who heard it knew that Princess Sparta was dead. It was the scream of a mother losing a child; it was the scream of loss of a loved one, and it would haunt the kingdom for years to come.

King Eurotas put on a brave face as Tiasa ran to try to console herself and her mother, but it was no use. Neither was capable of recovering from such a great loss, and the great king sat there alone by himself with Lacedaemon and his guards before him. "Thank you for all you have done, Lacedaemon. I appreciate your kind efforts in attempting to locate and recover my daughter. I am sorry you lost your future wife, and I wish you the best in pursuit of another," King Eurotas said with tears in his eyes.

Lacedaemon bowed before the king, and the next day, news was sent all over the kingdom and province of Laconia. The people left flowers and wreathes at the palace walls and gates. Many lit candles and said prayers as the grief was felt by everyone. This was not just the loss of the people's princess; it was the loss of a young girl who was practically still a child.

Though they had no body to bury, King Eurotas placed the bejeweled golden-cuffed bracelet and cloak into a chest carved with markings of the prestigious kind. Queen Clete placed more of Sparta's belongings into the chest, as did Tiasa, and slowly the chest was buried. It was Tiasa's idea to have the chest be buried before a willow tree that stood at the foot of the sea and a small garden built around it in memory of her sister.

The tall willow tree stood in enormity, and its large branches seemed to wrap around those who stood before it. Small bundles of pink flowers were placed over the newly dug earth, and the palace maidens had moved the tributes from the gates and gently put them here with care. For this was Sparta's final resting place; she always loved to climb this great willow that stood before the ocean since she was a child.

Lacedaemon and his guards watched as the royal family said their goodbyes and left together in tears. He hesitantly walked up and stood before the grave site. He placed a handful of bright fluorescent scarlet peonies onto the ground amongst the other flowers in solace for the loss of Sparta. "I'm sorry, I couldn't bring you home, and I'm sorry, I couldn't save you," Lacedaemon said quietly as a small tear fell from his left eye.

He stood up and breathed in as he stared at the massive willow tree that blew in the wind. The tall branches and leaves flowed through the wind like the ocean, and he understood why Sparta had liked it so much. His guards moved next to him and placed other items down for tribute and out of respect for the young girl who was lost to the sea.

They walked away together as other mourners came to pay their respects to the young princess. Lacedaemon and his guards walked past them, and seeing the people of Laconia lined up made Lacedaemon feel all the more guilty. He felt the weight of his actions sitting on his shoulders and wished he could go back and do things differently.

He wished he hadn't complained; he wished he wouldn't have prayed to his father; he wished that Sparta didn't die; and he wished she were still here. Lacedaemon wondered, how he could miss someone he hadn't even met, but seeing all of the people in the line who had tears pouring down their cheeks, and he heard the sniffles of their noses as they wiped them, he knew deep down how much Sparta had meant to the people. He could tell that she was the light of this kingdom that had now been snuffed out.

There was no going back and undoing what had already been done. Lacedaemon now had to live with his guilt forever, and although his future remained uncertain, he knew he would never take the same thing for granted again.

Chapter XII

Four Years Later…

Nerissa sunned herself on a flat rock as she and her sisters played in the ocean's waves. The sun's rays were firing down from the sky with such brightness and warmth that it made the sirens feel joyful. They braided their long, flowing hair and used sharp pieces of coral to rake their long locks into fine strands. While others splashed in the sea, and sunned themselves on other seaweed-covered rocks.

"I wish I were as beautiful as them," a voice said from behind Nerissa.

"You are, Sparta, you are," Nerissa replied, turning her neck to wave at the once young girl, who had now grown into a young woman sitting down next to her on the flat rock. Sparta sat next to Nerissa and lay stretched out on the rock as the sun beamed down onto them.

Nerissa looked at Sparta whose eyes were closed as she was taking in the warmth of the sun. She knew that it was almost time for the princess to leave this place, and deep down, she was going to miss her presence. In many ways, Nerissa felt like Sparta was her daughter. She had raised her to be strong and taught her how to survive. The two had bonded greatly, and Nerissa had taught her how to live like a siren.

Although the past four years were hard at times, Nerissa knew that the longer Sparta stayed here, the more she would forget who she really was. She did her best to remind the girl that she was the Princess of Laconia, but there were days that Sparta's memory would fade in and out.

The sirens did their best to bring back objects from the sea that would remind her of the life she used to have. Sparta remembered some things and parts of her life, but not all. She had come to outgrow her dress, and the sirens brought sails from a sunken ship that together they had fashioned into a makeshift dress. They braided her long, soft, chestnut-colored hair, and her skin grew sleek and soft. The more Sparta grew, the more the sirens saw her beauty, and the more they envied it. She was a true princess, beautiful inside and out.

Nerissa and her sisters had grown fond and protective of Sparta. They saw her as one of their own and told her stories of the sea. The ocean waves would roll in and out as the sirens dove through the waters, leading her to different parts of the land mass. They would watch the girl carefully, climb over the rocks, and run into the water to greet them each time they returned from a hunt. These were all the things each and every one of them would miss, especially Nerissa.

She had received a note from Poseidon, who had been given messages from the deities of prophecy, that it was almost time for Sparta to leave. Nerissa was told of a ship with big red sails and was given the description of a man who was supposed to find her. The sirens kept their eyes peeled for this ship and dreaded the day they would see it, but knew it was an order from a god that they could not disobey.

A chirp interrupted Nerissa's thoughts, and she looked over to her sister, who seemed panicked. A bunch of clicking noises began sounding and Nerissa sat up to look at what her sisters were going on about. In the distance, she could see a ship with big red sails and many other ships that trailed behind it.

Her sisters told her that there was a man who fitted the

description which Poseidon described, and with reluctance in her eyes, Nerissa woke up Sparta. "It's time for you to go," she said tearfully.

"Go where?" Sparta asked, confused.

"Go home," Nerissa replied.

"This *is* my home."

"It has been for the past four years, but it is time for you to return to your real home in Laconia."

"I don't understand," Sparta replied.

"You are Princess Sparta of Laconia, and you must return," Nerissa said adamantly.

"But I don't want to leave," Sparta replied, confused and a bit scared.

"You must," Nerissa said as she dragged Sparta off of the rocks into the waves.

Sparta fought hard to free herself from Nerissa, who emotionally dragged the princess through the waves. They arose to the surface, and the sirens held onto Sparta tightly as she frantically screamed for them to let her go. "I am sorry. Please, don't forget us," Nerissa said to Sparta.

"Let me go!" Sparta screamed. The ships began turning toward the sirens who were pushing Sparta further out to sea and toward the massive fleet. "Please!" Sparta screamed.

"Goodbye, little one," Nerissa said as she kissed Sparta on the cheek, and dove under water with her sisters to swim back toward the land.

Sparta struggled in the water, frantically searching for the sirens and Nerissa. "Are you all right, my lady?" a voice said from behind, and Sparta swiveled around to see a man standing on the bow of a ship. He reached down as the ships surrounded her on all sides, and used his great strength to pull her from the ocean and onto the deck. Sparta sat on the deck, confused and cold. "You're going to be all right," the man said as she stared into his dark but gentle brown eyes.

"Those damn sirens... always trying to drown people!" a guard said, handing Sparta a blanket to wrap around herself.

"They weren't trying to drown me, and don't you dare speak about them like that. They are my family!" Sparta replied in defense.

"You really must be delusional. How long have you been drifting?" a guard with blue eyes asked.

"I was not drifting. I live there," Sparta said, pointing back to the land she had called home for the past four years.

"She must've been shipwrecked and lived there for some time. I imagine she was trying to flee to us when the sirens tried to overtake her," another guard said with light blond hair.

"How she survived is a wonder, but you're lucky that we were here to save you," the man with brown eyes said.

"You did not save me! Now let me go!" Sparta yelled at him.

"We're headed to Ithaca. We'll let you go there," he replied.

Sparta stood and threw off the wool blanket. She darted for the side of the ship and tried to jump overboard, but the guard with blond hair grabbed her. "Let me go!" Sparta screamed.

"Tie her up so she doesn't try that again," the man with brown eyes ordered. The guards of the ship began tying her with ropes, and as hard as she fought, it was no use. They were stronger and bigger than she was. Sparta sat on the deck of the ship with her hands tied to her feet and her feet tied to the deck. She watched as the ships sailed in unison away from the place she knew as home.

Nerissa and her sisters rose to the surface and waved goodbye. Sparta cried and cried, but she knew it was no use. This really was a goodbye, and she would have to be brave in whatever and wherever she was headed. She looked up to see the big red sails catching the wind and saw a golden emblem that danced on the man with brown eyes' cape. The gold sigil against the red looked familiar to her, but she could not place it.

He held his hand on his sword, and Sparta watched the other guards march around the ship. She was angry and frustrated, but also sad. She had made up her mind that as soon as she was free, she was going to jump overboard, and if she couldn't, she would find a way to get back to the sirens.

The man with brown eyes looked at her as if he was only just seeing her for the first time.

"What's your name?" he asked, walking over to her.

"I'm not telling you," Sparta replied.

"Fine," he said, and walked back to his position of standing by the bow and looking toward the sea. The other guards eyed her intently, and all of them wondered who the strange girl they had found at sea was. Sparta could feel their eyes on her but knew it wasn't out of desire. She knew they were watching her to make sure she didn't try to jump overboard again. Sparta knew there was no escape to this ship and sat there with her arms wrapped around her legs as she tried to find comfort in herself but found none. All she could do was wait until they arrived at the destination they were sailing to, and she only hoped that she could remember her way back to the sirens.

Chapter XIII

Voyage to Ithaca

It had been sometime—weeks perhaps—since Sparta had been rescued from the ocean and placed onboard a ship full of men who were guards. She had learned that the man with the brown eyes was in charge of the fleet and the commander of all who surrounded him. She noticed his guards acted more like friends than the powerful, strong protectors they were dressed as.

The man with the brown eyes had tried to talk to her many times, and still Sparta refused to answer him. She had even refrained from speaking to him at all. Her feet and hands remained tied to the deck to prevent her from escaping, and while they fed her well and she happily ate, it did not console the emptiness she felt in her heart.

She still missed the sirens deeply, and although she liked hearing the stories the guards told, it was not the same as hearing the stories of the sea from Nerissa. Sparta had become accustomed to the routine of the ship and would watch the wind flow through the sails as seagulls soared from above. They must be close to land, but how close, she did not know.

How she yearned to be free, and the rope had begun itching her skin. She had scratched and pulled at the rope, but it only seemed to constrict itself tighter. It was no use, she knew, but she hoped that when they reached the land, she could commandeer a ship and sail back to the sirens and to the land she called home.

The ocean mist flew into her face as the waves became ever so choppy. The ships rocked and bounced up and down. The sea had grown restless, and the guards grabbed onto the frame of the steady ship to brace themselves. "Did you see that?" the guard with blue eyes asked.

"See what?" the man with the brown eyes answered. The ship jolted and almost tipped over as the guards were flung in the air, landing hard onto the deck. They stood quickly as the boat rocked back upright.

The ropes had prevented Sparta from swaying and being flung, but she fell sideways. She managed to catch her bearings as the ship turned upright, and she was frightened. The ships behind them began experiencing the same phenomenon as they were jolted and smacked around in the sea.

"What in the god's name?" the man with blond hair said, drawing his sword. All guards did the same, and even the man with brown eyes drew his blade, ready for whatever was going to happen next. There was silence, and the only noise Sparta could hear was that of the ocean's waves. The guards looked around attentive and cautious, ready to strike at any moment.

Their shields were risen to their chests and blades stuck out behind them. The ship jolted again, and this time, Sparta felt the strength of the jolt move through her. There was something below them, but no one dared look overboard. Could it be the sirens coming to rescue her? Sparta had to know, and she fought fiercely with the ropes to free herself.

A scream ripped from behind, and all heads turned backward. Sparta couldn't see what was going on behind her, but knew by the look on the faces of the strong men standing before her that it was one of pure terror. She could hear the ripping of wood being broken, torn, and cracked. It sounded familiar, and she knew she had heard that sound before, but could not remember from where.

"Steady yourselves!" the man with the brown eyes shouted.

"Light the torches; it doesn't like fire!" the guard with the blue eyes screamed. The ship jolted again, and the men were flung off their feet. One guard lost his dagger, and Sparta was able to grab it with both hands as she worked to free herself from the chains made of rope. The guards steadied themselves again as the boat rocked back into an upright position.

Sparta had worked through the ropes as a scream ripped through the air. It was not the scream of a man, but the scream of a monster. She stood up just as the massive beast was about to lunge toward their ship. Its spiny serpentine body was scaled with armor and had eyes that shone with the reddest fire. The sea serpent's teeth growled, and its body only grew taller as it emerged out of the water with such a power that terrified everyone with its enormity.

The sea beast lunged at the ship, and the guards readied themselves with arrows, torches, shields, and swords in hand. The beast towered down toward them but suddenly stopped. It looked at Sparta, who stared back at it with fear in her eyes, but as scared as she was, she did not look away. It lowered its head closer to Sparta, and she could feel its heat and power flare from its breath.

She remembered a story Nerissa had told her about the gatekeepers of the ocean. Tall, powerful, serpent-like beasts who lived in the oceans with daggers for teeth and fire for eyes. They were meant to guard Poseidon's treasure and kill all who sought to take it for their own.

Strong, formidable creatures that were monstrous in every way. Yet, the sea serpents had a job to do. Sparta knew how dangerous they could be, but she also understood their purpose. "Lower your weapons," Sparta said to the guards.

"Are you crazy?" the man with blue eyes yelled back.

"Lower your weapons!" Sparta yelled and dropped the blade in her hand.

"We will not!" the man with the brown eyes shouted back at her. The sea serpent let another scream rip from its throat, and the guards stood armed, ready to slay the monstrous beast, but Sparta remained calm. She stood there and, all at once, ran toward the bow of the ship and dived overboard. The sea giant plunged back into the ocean, leaving the guards dumbfounded.

The waters were quiet, and everything was calm again. The brave men looked at each other, puzzled, but did not lower their weapons or their guard. A scream could be heard from below the waters, and it rippled among the surface of the waves. The man with the brown eyes looked overboard cautiously and saw bubbles emerging from around the ship. He turned his head behind him to see most of his fleet still intact, but all of his guards still had their swords and shields at the ready.

The water burst with uproar as the giant sea serpent rose from the depths of the below. It surfaced with great propriety and towered once again over the ship. The guards were ready to strike but held their positions stunned at the sight they were seeing. Sparta clung go the sea beast's head as it rippled a scream out toward the ships. It slowly moved its head down toward the ship and Sparta fell off and onto the deck. The giant monster looked at her once again and then dove back into the sea. The man with the brown eyes knew that the sea serpent was done attacking, and he put his sword back into its sheath. The guards lowered their swords and shields, as they stood in awe of the girl standing before them.

"Who are you?" the man with the brown eyes asked, speechless.

"Wouldn't you like to know?" Sparta replied stubbornly.

The man scoffed in reply, and the ships began sailing again. The ocean was calm, and the waves remained peaceful as the sails were ignited with the wind to propel them forward once more.

The guards did not bother tying Sparta up again. She slowly walked toward the bow of the ship and stood next to the man with the brown eyes. "Why did you jump overboard and into the sea with that monster?" he asked her intently.

"I knew it wouldn't hurt me, and I only hoped it would take me back home," Sparta replied.

"Back to the sirens?"

"Yes."

"I don't know what happened to you, but I know that the sirens are not your home, and neither is that flat of sea sand," the man replied, referring to the beach Sparta called home.

"It is my home," she said persistently while wringing her hair of water.

"Where was your home before that home?" he asked, a bit frustrated.

"I don't remember," Sparta responded with disappointment.

"Of course, you don't," he replied, almost upset and bitterly at the same time.

Chapter XIV

Ithaca

The next afternoon arrived quickly, and the port of Ithaca came into view. Sparta could see every ship tied to the dock with their sails drawn in. She could see people working diligently, carrying crates of fish, and pulling at ropes. It was a busy place that had a familiar feeling to it, even though she was sure she had never been here before.

The fleet docked smoothly, and as soon as the ship was tied to the dock, the man with the brown eyes climbed down the wooden plank that was hoisted over the boat to create a bridge. His guards marched after him, and Sparta reluctantly followed. The salty sea air filled her nose, and the stench of fish smelled as they traveled further into the port.

There were people walking all about, and many sat before tables displaying all sorts of goods—from blankets, to wool, to jewelry, to netting, and even art work. Sparta was amazed at the variety of things she was seeing and the place felt enormous, even though it was small. The clouds moved with the wind above, and she followed the guards, not knowing where to go.

She desperately wanted to find a ship and make her way back to the sirens, but she also knew that it was impossible to do so. She felt like a child separated from her mother: scared, afraid, and unsure of what to do. Sparta trailed behind the flowing red capes of the guards who were in desperate need of a bath; she too needed one, she realized.

They came to a halt before a tall building with colossal towers and entered at will.

The walls were filled with various patterns of stories carved into the wood, and patterns of flowers swirled around the edges of the walls. The place had winding hallways, and kind women appeared to escort the guards into a room. They stopped Sparta and escorted her into a different one. It was here where she found a warm bath waiting for her.

The doors were closed, and she had the enormous room to herself. She quickly undressed and stepped into the bath that felt soothing in every way. She ran her fingers over her skin and used the cloth to scrub herself of dirt and ick that she had gathered from the ship. Sparta ran her fingers over the comb as she began diligently brushing her long, fine hair.

The doors opened, and a kind maid took her dress and brought her a new one. She smiled at Sparta, who smiled back to be friendly, but was a bit apprehensive to wear anything as dainty as what was laid out on the table in front of her. She dried herself quickly and slipped on the dress. It had a familiar feeling to it, and she twirled around the room feeling free and elegant.

Sparta peered out an opening in the wall and perched herself there, letting the wind dry her hair. She saw olive trees that were ripe for the picking and tall cypress trees that were a fruitful color of green. The mountains stood tall in the distance, and she could hear the bustling noise of the market by the port. It seemed so familiar, and Sparta began having faint glimpses of memories. She remembered a barrel of fish being spilled onto a dock and something about a tangerine. Maybe she was just imagining things, but it seemed so real.

Sparta put her thoughts behind her as the door opened and a maid escorted her out of the room. The white dress flowed at her feet, and the golden lace tied around the shoulders made her feel special and particularly beautiful.

The maid led her to a room where tables sat in a square and a man playing a lyre sat in the center. Sweet music filled the room, and all of the guards, who were now dressed in togas, sat with their swords at their sides and shoving their faces with food. The aroma of cooked meat and bread made her stomach growl.

She stood at the entrance and made her way to a chair next to the man with brown eyes. He was in deep conversation with a man next to him but held his cup of ale firmly. Although Sparta had often kept her distance from him, it was the first time she was able to accurately study his features. His smooth, tanned skin and arm muscles bulged in the golden cuffs placed around them. The darkness of his hair was ember brown, which flowed all the way down to his shoulders and had small ringlets of curls at the ends. His beard covered his face efficiently, but even through it, she could see his sharp jawline. The man was incredibly handsome, and it made Sparta feel a bit insecure about herself.

She ate the food placed in front of her contently, and when the man stopped strumming the lyre, everyone applauded. "A toast," an old man said, rising next to the man with the brown eyes. All held their cups up as he continued on to say something but stopped speaking when he saw Sparta. "And who might you be?" the old man asked curiously.

The man with the brown eyes turned to face Sparta and seemed to stare at her intently, as did the rest of the guards. She suddenly felt frazzled and nervous. The man with the brown eyes studied her before saying, "She was a girl we rescued at sea."

"How fortunate you are to be here. Your name?" the old man asked again, inquisitively. Sparta began to panic, but she remembered what Nerissa had told her. She looked at the old man and said, "My name is Princess Sparta of Laconia." The guard with the blue eyes spit his drink out of his mouth and began coughing abruptly.

"How funny you are. What is your real name?" the old man asked again.

"I just told you. I am Princess Sparta of Laconia," Sparta replied, confused.

"Princess Sparta of Laconia is dead," the guard with the blond hair said rather harshly. The old man looked at the man with brown eyes and said, "It seems Princess Sparta of Laconia is back from the dead. What wonderful news that is, Lacedaemon?"

The sarcasm in the old man's voice brought laughter to everyone and insult to Sparta. She had heard that name before, "Lacedaemon," and felt feelings of rage begin to boil within her.

"You shouldn't speak of the late Princess Sparta that way," the man with the brown eyes said.

"You are Lacedaemon?" Sparta asked, confused.

"I am," he replied before saying, "Who are you really?"

"I was supposed to marry you…" Sparta said as all the memories began coming back to her swiftly, and she suddenly felt overwhelmed.

"Plenty of women want to marry me, and I am more than used to it," he replied.

"No!" Sparta shouted before saying, "I was supposed to marry you." All eyes looked at her like she was crazy, and Sparta felt like a fool but didn't care.

"Tell me, how long was she out there? Long enough to lose her mind." the old man said and everyone laughed at her.

"Where is my bejeweled gold cuff?" Sparta said, looking at Lacedaemon. The laughter suddenly stopped.

"Your bejeweled gold cuff?" Lacedaemon replied, confused, still sitting and holding his cup of ale.

"And what happened to Philo and Sophus?"

"Who?" Lacedaemon asked.

"The boy who I gave the tangerine to and the skinny man in the white shirt who pulled me aboard his ship. Did they survive the storm?" Sparta asked Lacedaemon before going on to say, "And my cloak ripped off in Cythera..." Her thoughts began trailing off as she became consumed with memories and feelings of despair.

Lacedaemon looked at his guards, who were just as shocked. Sparta looked at him and darted toward the doors as he stood to run after her. "I will never marry you!" Sparta screamed down the halls. The guards intently followed as Sparta rushed outside and darted into the gardens. She could hear the footsteps of the men following her from behind, and it all suddenly felt so familiar.

Sparta remembered being chased by them at the port of Cythera and how she escaped the Kingdom of Laconia in order not to marry the man who was chasing her. *All of this to escape the man I was supposed to marry, only to be reunited with him again. This is certainly the gods' doing*, she thought to herself as she kept running, but Lacedaemon was fast on his feet.

Although in his mid-thirties, the man was spry and didn't have a single gray hair on his head or in his beard. His looks and youth prevailed as Sparta bent down to pick up a rock and throw it at him. It hit his head and bounced off, but he was in such close proximity to her that he was able to tackle her swiftly to the ground. Perhaps, her mistake was thinking that throwing a rock at a son of Zeus would stop him? It did not, and now she was captured.

Chapter XV

"Let go of me!" Sparta yelled at him. She clawed and tried to push him off of her, but it was no use. The man was too strong for her, and she knew it was pointless trying. Lacedaemon stood there, holding onto Sparta's arm, and began walking back the way they came through the gardens.

"Unhand me!" Sparta shouted at him as she stumbled alongside him.

"No," Lacedaemon replied calmly. It was only when he turned his head to look at her did Sparta see that the rock had struck him hard and blood dripped down the side of his face. She did feel bad about hurting him, but knew she did not want to be married to him. Her attempt to flee was not successful, but she was smart, clever even. She would find a way to escape and, once again, evade the man dragging her through the gardens.

"I said let go of me!" Sparta yelled again, and this time Lacedaemon released his grip and turned to Sparta. Lacedaemon looked at his guards, who understood he wanted privacy. They left politely, and he turned to her to say, "The entire Kingdom of Laconia and all of Greece believes you to be dead. And somehow you are alive and standing before me? Your family mourned you, all of Laconia mourned you. I, even, mourned you. Yet, here you are."

Sparta was left mostly speechless, but she managed to say, "I didn't know."

"Didn't know what?" Lacedaemon asked, fed up.

"That everyone thought I was dead," she replied quietly.

"Your ship went down in the 'sailor's doom.' We pulled the man in the white shirt out of the ocean, and we found your bejeweled gold cuff tied up with a sail. My men and I searched the water for hours, looking over every piece of wreck from that ship. We never found you, but now it's clear why. You somehow survived," said Lacedaemon.

"The sirens saved me and dragged me to shore. I didn't ask to be saved, but someone commanded it."

"We sailed by that flat of sand, and you never once called out to us. It's clear to me that you would've rather stayed on that rocky shore forever than to marry me," Lacedaemon said a bit broken hearted.

"I was just a child, and like I said, I was ordered to stay there. The sirens would've drowned me if I had tried to leave," Sparta replied, trying to defend her point of view.

"I don't believe you or any of what you are saying. You've insulted me, and when all of Laconia finds out you are alive, you'll have to beg your father for forgiveness for what you've done," Lacedaemon said angrily.

"I regret nothing, and I won't beg for forgiveness because I'm not going back,"

"I am bringing you back myself."

"You'll try," Sparta said, testing Lacedaemon's patience.

"Kleon!" Lacedaemon shouted, and Sparta watched the blond-haired man run to greet them.

"Yes."

"Take her to her room and make sure guards stand there all night. We leave tomorrow morning for Laconia," Lacedaemon ordered.

"As you wish," Kleon replied, as he grabbed Sparta who

looked behind her to see Lacedaemon sternly staring at her. She was dragged back into the building and placed in a room with a small bed. A candle had been lit as dusk had now settled in, and it sparked light in the room. The shadows danced as Sparta sat on her bed, crying. *I will get out of this. I must*, she thought to herself.

She looked around the room and saw a window placed almost as high as the ceiling. There was no way she could get up there and climb out without hurting herself. The guards placed at her door hadn't moved just as Lacedaemon ordered. Sparta thought of trying to convince the guards to go get her something, but she knew they were not going to budge or leave their post at her door.

There was only one option: the window. *But how to get up there?* she thought. Sparta began stripping the sheets of her bed and tying one after the other to fashion herself a long chain of cloth. The sailor's knot she had learned had come in handy, and she knew it would hold her weight. All she had to do was somehow get it all the way up and out the window, along with herself.

Sparta looked around the room frantically for something heavy that she could attach the long string of cloth to. She found nothing, but maybe she didn't need something heavy to throw out the window as a weight. Instead, she could climb the wall. It would be risky, but there were small indents that showed wear and tear. No one had bothered fixing the chips or crevices that had formed with age. She heaved the blanket of tied cloth around her shoulders and carefully began scaling the large wall.

It was harder than she expected, but she took her time. Her toes felt for crevices to propel her upward, and her hands searched for edges to grasp. She slowly forced herself upward and toward the window. The weight of the sheets were heavy on her shoulders, and it made her feel exhausted, but Sparta would not give up.

Her hands finally reached the window's opening and with one heave of strength, she pulled herself upward. She sat on the window sill and began taking the cloth off her shoulders, breathing heavily as she did so. Sparta let the string of sheets and blankets unravel before her, down the side of the building. She managed to use her fingers to wiggle one of the heavy bricks out from its place in the wall. Its weight almost caused her to fall off the window sill, but she breathed in heavily and hoisted it up in her lap. The cloth wrapped around it with ease, and she began making her way down the side of the building.

Her feet hit with a "thud," and she looked up, proud at her escape. Sparta turned around, and her jaw fell open. "I was wondering if you were bold enough to try that," Lacedaemon said, standing before her.

Sparta was left shocked and now utterly frustrated. "You said everyone thinks I'm dead. Let me go and everyone can keep thinking that. You and I will live out our lives, never seeing one another again," she said, desperately hoping he would agree to the deal.

"Are you begging me to let you go, Princess?" Lacedaemon asked intently.

"I'm asking you to let me go," she replied.

"I made a promise to your father to wed you. I gave my word then, and it still stands now," Lacedaemon said stubbornly.

"Why me? Why would you want to marry me?" Sparta asked emotionally.

"I didn't know you were a child at that time. Your father never told me that when he offered your hand in marriage to me," he replied, a bit upset that he had been deceived.

"If you let me go, you can wed any woman of your choosing."

"I gave my word."

"I will not marry you."

"I'm afraid you must," Lacedaemon said as the air around them turned heavy. Sparta could feel the tears swelling in her eyes, but she used her strength to hold them in. They stared at each other for some time, not knowing what to say about the predicament they were both in. Lacedaemon had been deceived and lied to by King Eurotas, all in order to gain his word to wed Sparta, who was just a child, years ago. He looked at the princess before him, who was holding back tears with all her strength. Perhaps he should let her go. No one would have to know, but to go against his word would be wrong. It was a promise that could not be broken, and morally, it would go against everything Lacedaemon stood for.

He looked at Sparta again, whose eyes pleaded with him. She was no longer the child he had chased in Cythera; she was now a young woman, who he realized was quite beautiful. He recognized Queen Clete's eyes in hers and could see she had the color of King Eurotas's hair.

She was radiant in every way, just as he had been told all those years ago, but now, to see her radiance with his own eyes only made him feel all the worse for what he must do. "I truly am sorry, Princess. I cannot break my word to your father. We will leave tomorrow for Laconia, and we will be wed," he said, feeling guilty inside.

Sparta pondered with what Lacedaemon had said to her. She was upset but would not show it. She didn't want to give him any satisfaction to how she was feeling. "There must've been a reason you came here?" she asked, changing the topic of the conversation.

"There was, but it does not matter now. Plans have changed," Lacedaemon replied.

"What were you here for?" Sparta asked again.

"We were to march to Dodona. There is rumor of war stirring about, and Thessalia is eager to expand its territories," he said, a bit disappointed.

"Dodona? I recall learning about that place. It is said to have a connection with your father, Zeus," Sparta replied, displaying her educational abilities.

"Yes, it is, and I wish to go help defend it; war would break out, but I'm afraid, I cannot do that anymore. We need to get you back to Laconia."

"Or we could go to Dodona and help defend it. For your father and the people, of course," Sparta replied hoping Lacedaemon would consider her proposal.

"We will go back to Laconia."

"If you try to take me back to Laconia, I will make it very difficult for you. However, I offer you a choice. I can make things unpleasant, or we can go to Dodona, and once we are done helping there, we will return to Laconia, and I will marry you," Sparta said, with great strength behind her voice.

"You will marry me if we go to Dodona?" Lacedaemon asked, confused.

"Yes."

"You won't try to escape or run away?"

"I will not. I give you, my word," Sparta replied.

"And when we are done, we sail back to Laconia and wed?" Lacedaemon asked.

"Yes."

He breathed in, contemplating Sparta's offer and thinking about what he should do. Lacedaemon looked at Sparta, and he knew deep down that the girl was stalling. She wanted to go to Dodona in order to not go to Laconia. Sparta had given her word that she would not try to escape or run away, but he didn't believe her. He felt that somehow she was going to find a way out of this, and the princess had made it obvious that she would do anything in order not to marry him.

"Give me your word; that the entire time we travel to Dodona, are at Dodona, and travel back to Laconia, you will not try to escape, or run away, or jump overboard. Your word, Sparta!" Lacedaemon said sincerely.

"I give you my word that I will not try to escape, run away, or jump overboard the entire time we travel to Dodona, are at Dodona, and on our journey back to Laconia. I will not make things difficult, and I will listen to your every command," she replied with truth in her voice, but Sparta had a plan of escape and Lacedaemon knew.

Chapter XVI

The next morning, Sparta arose from her sleep and rubbed her eyes with her hands. She saw the light break through the window in rays of golden sunshine. Her feeling of contentment beamed, and she was glad to not go back to Laconia anytime soon. She had a plan, or at least a part of one. Though she had given Lacedaemon her word, she knew there was a way out.

Sparta would continue to think about her plan every day until she needed to escape. She would honor her word until that day came. For now, a maid came through the doors and placed a platter of cheese, fruit, bread, and drink at the end of her bed. Sparta thanked the woman and ate diligently. She dressed and ventured out into the hall, only to be stopped by the guard with blue eyes.

"Princess Sparta," he said.

"And which one are you?" she asked him.

"Nicander," he replied.

"Nice to meet you. Lacedaemon uses so many names, I never know which of you is which," she said with a bit of laughter in her voice.

Sparta watched Nicander smile before saying, "This way."

She followed Nicander down winding hallways, and they came to a room. Lacedaemon and the rest of his guards were dressed in their uniforms. The gold plates of armor that covered their chests had been cleaned and shimmered in the light. The red capes that carried a gold emblem flowed behind every step they took. The gold cuffs around their arms made their muscles bulge, and their sandals were strapped tightly to their feet.

Lacedaemon had his hand on his sword and was speaking with his guards about the travel to Dodona. He had a strategy, and the more Sparta listened to him express his knowledge, the more she realized his intelligence. The man would not be easy to fool, and Sparta knew this made her escape all the more challenging. He would keep an eye on her every step of the way, and she knew he would keep her close to him. This only made her plan more complicated, but she was not one to give up or back down from a difficult task at hand.

*

The journey to Dodona was long, and it would all be on foot. They would scale rocky peaks and walk through the summer's heat. Every day would bring a new challenge, physically and mentally, but Sparta was determined. Lacedaemon had told her that if they kept up the pace he had set for them each day, they should reach Dodona's capital by the next full moon.

She knew it would be a difficult trek, but she strapped her sandals on her feet and prepared herself for the adventure ahead. The guards followed Lacedaemon and marched in rows of three.

Sparta was to stay next to him, and Nicander closely walked by her other side. She was boxed in between the two men, and she knew this was Lacedaemon's doing.

They walked at a fast and steady pace, and Sparta found it hard to keep up since she was not as tall as the men beside her or marching behind her. Her feet occasionally stumbled over one another, and there were times where she almost tripped. Lacedaemon eyed her carefully and pressed on despite her clumsiness.

The guards carried shields on their backs, and the soldiers that followed carried their weapons with great care. They found shelter under some trees and stopped to rest for a moment. Sparta washed her feet in the small brook that flowed in tranquility. Her sandals had blistered her ankles and rubbed the skin off her toes.

The water stung, but the coolness of it relieved the burning sensation she felt. Sparta continued to soak her feet in the brook and turned to see Lacedaemon keeping a watchful eye on her. She took a sip of her water from its pouch and was about to stand when he placed his hand on her shoulder, forcing her to sit back down.

"Here," he said, handing her a piece of a plant before saying, "Rub it on the wounds on your feet. It should help with the pain,"

Sparta looked at him and said, "Thank you."

He nodded his head and went back to stand under the tree with his guards. They chatted amongst themselves as Sparta split open the plant to see its fine sap ooze in her hands. She carefully rubbed the golden-colored sap on her wounds and rinsed her hands in the creek.

The guards had started marching again, and Sparta was quick to take her place back between Lacedaemon and Nicander. She placed her sandals in her bag and walked barefoot along the path. The rocks were pointy under her feet, but she did not wince or complain. She distracted herself by looking at her surroundings; the sky was filled with white cotton clouds, and the bushes they passed by were flowering colors of pink and yellow. Their scent filled her nose as she walked by them, and she smiled at the sweet smell.

They had reached the beach, and Sparta could see small rowboats ready and waiting. In the distance, she saw land and knew that's where they were headed. The maps she had seen in Laconia charted a small break of ocean between Ithaca and Dodona. She had remembered this and many other details about Dodona that had resurfaced from her memory.

Lacedaemon offered a hand to help her into the small rowboat, and she accepted. The guards began rowing, and the fleet of small boats took off together, paddling toward the shores of Dodona. The waterway was narrow, and the turquoise waves flowed past them easily. Sparta looked down to see the sands fading from her view, and below them, a deep, dark crevice emerged. It scared her to look at the vastness of it, and she looked up at Lacedaemon, who offered her a stern look as he rowed on.

The rowboats hit the shores with a jolt that almost knocked Sparta backward. She climbed out quickly, as did the rest of the guards, and soon they began wading into the thicket of the forest-like jungle. The trees were tall, and the grass rose to her height. The noise of the ocean faded, and branches began snapping under her feet.

Sparta had never seen scenery quite like this. The trees had jade leaves, and their branches extended out to touch other trees. The ground was hard and covered in brown earth. There were insects that flew around her head, and she tried swatting them away with her hand but whacked Lacedaemon in the face instead. She offered a smile of apology as he offered a look of frustration.

Sparta knew his patience for her was thin, and it seemed all of the guards and soldiers felt the same. No one would even care to look at her, and when the sun began setting, they settled under a thicket of oak trees. The fire was ignited by a man with rowdy hair and a small beard, growing

from his chin that she had come to know as Basilius. His focus remained on the fire as many of the soldiers and guards stood by, drinking cups of ale while chewing on bits of bread.

She turned her head to see Lacedaemon and Nicander returning with a handful of rabbits. They were skilled hunters, and Kleon returned from another direction with a mound of fish filling his basket. The men skewed and gutted each animal before placing its meat on sticks to be cooked around the fire.

Sparta was unsure of where to make herself useful and felt very alone in the midst of all of these men. She sat on her blanket and wrapped another around herself. The bread in her bag was hard, but the cheese was still fresh. She ate it while turning her back to the guards and looked out into the distance.

Her hands wrapped around her knees inside the blanket, and she placed the rest of her food back into her bag. "Here," a voice said from behind. Lacedaemon knelt down and sat next to her. He handed her a stick of cooked meat and used his knife to scrape the tender meat off of his.

"Thank you," Sparta said to him, eating the meat happily.

"You're welcome," he replied.

The two sat there not speaking, and ate their share of the meat. The awkwardness between them was seen by everyone. Lacedaemon was always unsure of what to say or how to read the girl sitting next to him. She was a mystery, even though he knew so much about her. All of the things he was told and all he had learned could not have prepared him for the young woman sitting next to him. The princess had changed in more ways than one, and all he was told did not matter anymore. He was sitting next to a stranger he did not know, even though he did.

Sparta felt the same and could see Lacedaemon staring at her, and she only wondered, what he was thinking. It felt strange to sit so close to the man she resented so much. She kept her gaze ahead of her and thought about him. He was the man she had never met before, but now she had, and she knew nothing about him. All she knew was what her tutor and maids had told her all those years ago. The son of Zeus and a mighty warrior was all she could remember, as she tried to forget most details of him at the time.

She found him to be intriguing and entertaining in a way that sparked her curiosity. The man was steadfast, strategic, stoic, mighty, and quite handsome, but Sparta was not about to let any emotion get the best of her. He had chased her in Cythera, found her on the flat of sand, taken her away from the sirens, tied her to a ship, sailed her to Ithaca, and even prevented her escape. She hated him with every piece of her being, but she was also fascinated by him, the son of Zeus.

Chapter XVII

Journey to Dodona

The next few days had the same routine. They woke up and began marching as soon as the sun rose over the peaks. Their pace was fast and breaks were short. They would find a thicket of trees to camp against each night, and the guards would take turns hunting or foraging for food. Sparta made herself useful by collecting wood and sticks where she could to keep the fire burning at night.

She still felt out of place, and the guards had refrained from speaking to her at all. The loneliness had settled in, and as emotional as she felt, she knew she needed to keep herself together. It was her suggestion to go to Dodona in order to not go to Laconia, but she hadn't thought the whole thing through. She hadn't counted on the heat-filled days and the aches in her feet.

For the time she survived and lived with the sirens on her own, it seemed easy, but this was nothing short of simple. Sparta was not a guard or a soldier. She was a princess who was not as tall, strong, built, or as battle ready as the men who surrounded her. They were built like bulls and had been trained for war. All of them were used to marching at great distances and she was not.

She knew the guards saw her as a dead weight, and sometimes the wind would blow their conversations in her direction. Sparta could hear them speaking about her unkindly and it only made her feel worse. She was only here because Lacedaemon ordered it and that was the truth.

This is what she overheard the guards discussing, that or her identity. Some thought she was a fake, but the ones closest to Lacedaemon knew it was really her, and they hushed the ones who questioned otherwise. Her feet ached, and she sat there in the quiet of the night, rubbing them. She thought of stories Nerissa told her to take her mind off of where she really was.

Sparta lay down and wrapped herself in a blanket. She could hear the guard's boisterous laughter from behind her but looked up at the stars to find solace. They shimmered and shined as she tried to find every constellation that was high up in the charcoal-colored sky. Her eyes grew tired, and she drifted into sleep.

The crickets chirping awoke Sparta from her dreams. The darkness surrounded her, and she could see nothing. The fire had faded out, and no light could be seen except for the stars that gleamed from above. A stick snapped from behind her. Sparta froze in her blanket as her heart beat faster and faster.

She felt someone suddenly grasp her, and a hand fell over her mouth.

"*Shhhh...*" Lacedaemon whispered into her ear. Sparta kept herself still, as she was unsure why he had come to wake her during such late hours. When her vision finally adjusted to the darkness, she could see that none of the guards were sleeping. They were all behind Lacedaemon, crouched down with their swords drawn.

Sparta sat up quietly, and Lacedaemon pushed himself in front of her. Together, the guards and soldiers edged back behind the thicket of trees. Kleon grabbed Sparta's hand and pulled her down behind a tree as Lacedaemon stood next to her. She could see the light of the stars glimmering off of their shields that were drawn at the ready, and their swords sparkled in the light of the night.

Sparta felt panicked but calm at the same time. "What's

going on?" she wanted to ask Lacedaemon, but knew she needed to be quiet. This was no time for questions or chit-chat. There was a clear presence of danger in the air, and Sparta felt it creep its way toward her. The chill of the mist touched her skin and gave her goosebumps. The humidity in the air was thick but had a coldness to it. It filled her lungs refreshingly, but also made her feel on edge.

The "clip clopping" of horse hooves could be heard in the distance as a small flock of men emerged from across the field and rode toward their camp by the thicket of trees. Sparta could see that most of the blankets had been taken away or concealed to make it appear as a small battalion camping rather than a big one.

A man in a silver helmet jumped off his horse and touched the coals of the fire. "They were here," he said in a deep voice. The other riders began sweeping the forest line, searching for them. Sparta kept her head down and back against the tall tree they were hiding behind. The others did the same, and the man on the horse did not see them. "They couldn't have gotten far," the man in the silver helmet said before climbing back onto his horse.

He began riding straight toward the forest as his group of soldiers followed him. They rode fiercely, and the minute they rode past Lacedaemon and his guards, the groups began attacking one another; six men on horses against all of the soldiers Sparta was hiding with was not a fair battle at all. She cowered behind the tree as the men launched at each other, and she saw the man in the silver helmet's head roll off his body. His horse was grabbed by Lacedaemon, and Sparta watched as blood was spilled in the darkness of the night.

It all happened so fast, as the guards had grabbed the horses that stomped on the bodies of their dead riders. Lacedaemon emerged from the forest with Nicander at his side, and his guards began marching back toward the camp. They had reached the fire pit when another man on a horse revealed himself with a bow and arrow.

He began charging on his horse toward Lacedaemon and the guards, but Sparta quickly grabbed the spear from Basilius's hand and launched it at the man before he could fire his arrow. The spear struck his torso, and he fell off the horse as she grabbed its reins to stop it from running off. She stroked the spooked horse's face, and it calmed down at her gentleness.

"Where did you learn to do that?" Lacedaemon asked, a bit speechless.

"The sirens taught me how to spear fish," Sparta replied with a bit of a smile.

Lacedaemon smiled back before saying, "Pack everything up and hide their bodies as best you can. We need to move, now!"

The guards and the soldiers worked quickly to hide all traces that they were there. Sparta hoisted herself on top of the gentle horse, as Lacedaemon did the same to his horse. The other five horses were ridden by Nicander, Kleon, Basilius, Callias, and another young soldier named Lysander. Sparta figured he had been well liked by Lacedaemon if he was now riding with the higher guards, who were more like friends than strong brutes designed for war.

The sun had risen slowly from the east, and its rays shined in the leaves of the trees they marched past. They were entering the mountains, and Sparta could see a river flowing ahead. It was when they had stopped to rest, that she found the courage to ask Lacedaemon who those men were who attacked them.

"Those men. Who were they?" she asked him as they sat

down by the river together.

"Scouts from Thessailia," he replied, drinking from his pouch of water.

"Are you certain?"

"Yes."

"How do you know for certain they are from Thessailia?"

"Because I have fought Thessalian men before," Lacedaemon said looking down at his feet.

"You have?" Sparta replied curiously.

"Yes. They are strong, but reckless and impulsive when it comes to battle. I have beat them before."

"I knew you had fought battles before, but I wasn't aware one was with Thessailia," Sparta said, as Lacedaemon clicked his tongue in his mouth before saying, "It was a naval battle off the coast of Delfi, but they went inland, and we followed. We were able to push them back into their territory."

"This seems like an ongoing war," she said, a bit puzzled.

"It has been ongoing for the past four years," he replied, a bit exhausted.

"Did it have anything to do with me dying?" Sparta asked, feeling a bit guilty about everything.

"Unfortunately, 'your death' and my failure to marry you did start this whole predicament."

"How so?" Sparta asked.

"My marriage to you was political, and for me to secure allegiance with Laconia was to signify and strengthen my allegiance to Dodona, and all of the bordering provinces. Our union would have demonstrated the uniting of Dodona and Laconia. Thus, proving us to be a formidable ally and threat to all surrounding us," Lacedaemon said while fumbling with his sword.

"It's just politics, isn't it?" Sparta responded, sounding disappointed.

"It always has been, and you know that. Your supposed 'death' showed weakness for Laconia and Dodona. Thessalia has seen an opportunity to exploit it and seeks to gain more territory. I must not allow that to happen," he replied, sounding determined but also a bit sad.

"I truly am sorry," Sparta said with sincerity, not realizing how her actions of running away had caused so much damage.

"As am I," Lacedaemon responded, standing up and walking over to go speak with his ring of higher trusted guards. She had learned that he picked a select few to entrust duties to and those standing around him; Kleon, Basilius, Callias, Nicander, and Lysander, were whom he trusted most. They were in charge of the other guards or soldiers. She was never sure which to refer to them by, since they were all dressed the same.

Sparta thought about what Lacedaemon had said, "politics"—that was all this marriage was, and it opened her eyes to the reality of what she had run away from. She ran away from a man she did not know or wish to marry, but in the process, she allowed her country and Lacedaemon to fall under attack. Her actions had endangered the lives of everyone, and she felt selfish for running away from it. However, she was just a child and too young to understand the realities of politics that surrounded her. After all, no one had told her what would happen if she did not marry him. Sparta was now seeing the consequences of her actions, and she began to regret her decision.

Chapter XVIII

The air was dense, and the terrain was rocky as they trekked on through the mountains. The birds chirped and flew by them, darting into pine trees. The tall, evergreen trees were as high as the sky, and it seemed as if they could almost touch the clouds. The wind blew a gentle breeze that made waves in Sparta's hair as Lacedaemon rode next to her.

His focus was steady on the path ahead, and Nicander rode on the other side of her. They still didn't trust her to not escape again, but things had changed. Sparta now understood her responsibilities, which she hadn't understood before and had come to a realization of what it really meant to be a princess. Her country comes first, the people second, and everything else last. It no longer mattered what she wanted for herself; she had a duty to fulfill, and she would not fail.

She let her plan of escape fall from her thoughts and mind. Sparta had never understood her father's reasoning for things but now it all became clear: it was politics. Lacedaemon had explained that to her, and she had come to understand it as a game. The right decisions and unity demonstrate strength, but the wrong decisions demonstrate weakness. If weakness was shown, suffering followed, and not onto her but onto the people of Laconia. The people were hers: to protect, to love, and to take care of.

It was in this realization that Sparta had come to find a sense of maturity within herself and a power deep in her soul that she never recognized before. She felt strong and finally understood all of her father, the great King Eurotas's, decisions. Her mother had been there idly by his side all these years to support his decisions and offer insight. Sparta remembered overhearing conversations they had about battle, strategy, the kingdom, and other endeavors.

She replayed much of it in her mind and understood not only what a king's duty is but what a queen's duty is as well. Sparta had never seen these qualities displayed in Tiasa and felt that perhaps this was why the focus of marriage was on her. She had the potential to become the great diplomat that her father and mother had wanted her to be, even if they did not openly tell her at the time.

That potential had grown, and Sparta knew she must live up to it. She had survived for a reason, and even though it was due to someone's command—a god, she figured—she was thankful. It was a second chance that she would not fail at and strive for success. She would make sure that Thessalia did not win this war, and she would also protect the man riding next to her at any cost necessary. Though she still did not like him, she tolerated him, and that was enough. "Politics," she kept reminding herself, and everything I do from now on will be for Laconia and its people, my people. It was this new-found sense of confidence that made Sparta smile, and Lacedaemon saw.

He knew something had shifted in the girl he was riding next to. Maybe that talk by the river had made her understand her actions and the consequences of them. He believed that she did not fully consider what running away had done and what her "death" had caused. Lacedaemon wondered what she was thinking about, and some part of him hoped she thought of him.

They camped under a grove of fir trees that were dense and

thick. The fire was small but provided enough flame to cook game the men hunted. The guards were now speaking to Sparta, and she felt included for the first time. She believed this was due to her spearing the man with the bow and arrow, who charged them the night before.

The guards all continued their banter as others sharpened their swords with rocks they found lying around. Sparta walked to the edge of the thicket and sat there, staring at the view. They were high up in the mountains, and the moon glowed from above, showing the shadows of many trees and tall peaks in the distance. The stars twinkled and glistened as the wind rattled through the branches of the furs.

Lacedaemon came to sit next to her, and Sparta had gotten used to his presence. She did not feel as insecure or frightened of him as she used to. The man had a charm to him, and it was alluring. She found it almost impossible not to allow some part of her to like the great son of Zeus sitting next to her.

In their time of traveling together, she had come to recognize his facial expressions, and it helped her understand his temperament. She picked up the slightest raise of his shoulders and tension in his muscles. He was nervous to be sitting next to her, or maybe he was just tense from the journey they were embarking on. She said nothing, and the two sat together in complete silence.

"It's quite beautiful," Lacedaemon said, finally breaking the silent awkwardness.

"Yes, it is," Sparta replied, staring up at the stars.

"You like the stars?" he asked.

"I would stare at them every night out of my window in Laconia," Sparta said with a bit of a smile, remembering the view.

"Your window faced the sea. I can imagine the view at night was quite extraordinary."

"How do you know about the view from my window?"

"I did search the entire palace for you," Lacedaemon said with a laugh. Sparta laughed too before saying, "The whole palace, really?"

"Yes, really. General Adamantios was convinced that someone had helped you escape. He interrogated everyone," Lacedaemon replied, remembering moments from all those years ago.

"No one helped me to escape," Sparta replied.

"Oh, I know. You slipped through your door at night, since you timed the guards' patrols and jumped over the wall, ran to the port, stole a small rowboat, and rowed to Cythera," he said with a laugh.

Sparta laughed hard before saying, "Well... anything to not marry you."

Lacedaemon laughed as the two stared at each other before he asked, "What really happened to you? How did you survive the 'sailor's doom'?"

"I remember we did not sail into the storm. The storm sailed into us, and I remember hearing the ship crack. I was flung overboard and held onto a barrel for my life. I thought I was going to die. The waves kept pushing me under, and everything went black. I woke up on that flat of sand, and Nerissa explained to me that they had been ordered to save me."

"Who is Nerissa?"

"The siren who saved me. She told me that if I tried to leave, the sirens would drown me. I was to remain there until they were told otherwise. I figured it was punishment for not marrying you and running away," Sparta replied steadily.

"A punishment from the gods?" Lacedaemon asked, a bit perplexed.

"I did run away from marrying a son of Zeus," Sparta said with a laugh.

Lacedaemon smiled before saying, "Four years?"

"I don't really recall for how long I was there. It was hard to remember things like time or memories of where I came from. I think that's why it took me so long to remember you and who I was," she replied to him.

"Makes sense," he said.

"I guess I ran away only to run into you again."

"Certainly, the gods' doing," Lacedaemon said with a smile. He stared into Sparta's iridescent eyes and found himself mesmerized by her. Though it was dark, he could still see the hues of faint blue and green that seemed to dance in a collage of beauty among her eyes. He was entranced.

"I should get to sleep," Sparta said, breaking the connection as she stood up to walk back to the camp.

"Yes, of course," Lacedaemon said as he stood up and followed Sparta back to the camp.

*

Sparta felt the rain before she saw it. It woke her up from the deep sleep she was enjoying, and she stared up to see the ash gray clouds letting water release from the heavens. The guards were already awake and packing up their belongings. She rose quickly and began tying her belongings to her horse, whom she'd grown quite fond of.

"I shall call you Asterius," she whispered into the black stallion's ear, and he bucked, eager to receive a name worthy of his might and beauty. Sparta petted the gentle horse, who welcomed her soft touch with snorts and playful noises. She laughed quietly to herself at the horse's character and wit.

"I think he likes you," Lacedaemon said, hopping up onto his horse.

Sparta smiled and replied, "Yes, yes, he does." She pulled herself up onto the mighty horse and patted his head again as the guards readied to march. Her head turned around, and it was the first time she really understood how big of a battalion she was in front of. The line of men reached beyond her view and back into the trees. This was a small army, but one big enough to scare anything in its path with its numbers and intimidating soldiers.

They set out on a steady pace, and the mountains grew more rugged with each step. It took a full week before they were out of the steep peaks and forest that covered the tall summit. It had rained most of the time which did not make the long trek any faster, but suddenly, the terrain changed.

The path became flat and the grasslands emerged as they left the ragged mountains behind. Sparta looked behind her to see the tall, pointed caps become dots in her view. The olive-green grass frolicked in the wind, and it was a beautiful place. There were wildflowers blooming in the fields of orange, yellow, white, gold, and some even pink. Sparta could smell the daisies in the wind, and everything around them was peaceful.

The smooth path allowed them to make up the lost time, and the full moon finally arrived. They had reached the capital of Dodona. The city came into view, and Sparta could see the theater filled with people cheering and calling out chants of encouragement. She could see people waving at them as they carried baskets of fruit on their heads.

The place was large but small at the same time. They passed

by various buildings made of stone, and children played in the road but moved as they marched by. Everyone stopped to stare, and many whispered or waved. Sparta could see many women staring at Lacedaemon and waving at him. He offered a smile and a wave back.

They dismounted their horses and were greeted by the general of the Dodona army. He escorted the soldiers to another building while Lacedaemon and his ring of guards were invited into another. Sparta followed, eager to see inside the beautiful building before her. She stepped a foot inside and was immediately seized by two women who escorted her to a room.

It was there she bathed, dressed, and ate quickly. She stepped outside of the room to see three women surrounding Lacedaemon. One was stroking his arm and running her hands over his muscles. The other was twirling her hair and batting her eyes at him. While the last one was running her hand up and down his chest. He did not push them away or even stop their flaunting with him. If anything, he welcomed it.

Chapter XIX

Sparta turned away, angry. She walked quickly outside and found a tall willow tree to sit under. It reminded her of the one she used to play in as a child. The tall branches that stretched far and wide, with their leaves blowing in the wind elegantly. She wanted to cry but refrained from wasting her tears.

"Lacedaemon was nothing to cry over," she told herself, but found she was hot with anger. Sparta had come to like him as much as she resented him. The man had a way about him, and jealousy boiled through her veins. "You ran off?" a voice said from behind her. She said nothing as Lacedaemon came to sit next to her.

"You seemed busy," she replied bitterly.

"How so?" Lacedaemon replied arrogantly.

Sparta was mad at his response but understood that, although he was joking, he was not at the same time. He knew of his beauty and his charm. The man used it to his advantage, and she realized that he wanted her to be jealous. She was playing right into his hand, and he smiled at her, knowing he had gotten what he wanted.

"They were just teasing me," he said to her, trying to get her to talk, but Sparta did not feel like talking. She sat here in silence, contemplating what to do next. "I'm not interested in them, if that's what you're wondering," he said, realizing his mistake.

"You seemed quite interested, and we're not married yet. I suppose you can run off with whatever whore you want," she replied harshly to him.

"Really?" he said sarcastically, and Sparta looked at him with hateful eyes.

"If that's what you wish," she replied, holding back her emotions with all her strength.

"What if it isn't what I wish?" he asked.

"Then, I do not know what you want," Sparta said.

Lacedaemon placed a hand on her chin and turned her head toward his. He kissed her deeply and intimately, savoring the taste of her lips on his. Sparta leaned away, and although she liked the feeling of his lips on hers, it did not change what she had seen moments ago. She looked at him hard and slapped him in the face.

Lacedaemon looked at her, stunned, as she got up to walk away from him. "Sparta!" he yelled, but she did not turn around. She did not want him to see her cry or how upset she was. Her legs broke out into a sprint, and she ran faster and faster. A part of her hoped he was chasing after her like he had all of those times before, but another part of her also hoped he would leave her to be on her own.

She ran past the jade-colored grass and through a field of cypress trees. The hill was steep, but she ran up it and hid herself behind one of the tall cypress trees. Her legs fell beneath her, and she fell into a ball on the ground. Sparta let herself sob and cry. It was at that moment that she realized all possibilities of even allowing her mind to wonder and think about the feelings she was having for Lacedaemon had turned to hate.

The man was untrustworthy, and she knew he would never look at her the way he looked at those other women. She was just the girl he was promised to marry, and nothing more. Although she was a princess, it did not change how she felt inside. She felt she was not as beautiful or as enticing as those women who had surrounded Lacedaemon. Sparta had always been told of her beauty, but she questioned it now more than ever. How could he not see her? How could he not like her? What was so bad about her?

She quickly realized she needed to stop thinking that way. There was nothing wrong with her, and she was beautiful in every way. If Lacedaemon could not see it, then she was his loss. Sparta wanted more than ever to run away and never see him again. However, she knew Laconia came first, and maybe she could find a way to not marry him but also stop the war between Dodona and Thessalia.

Sparta wiped her tears and sat up to look down the hill she had run up. The grass flowed in the wind and Lacedaemon had not chased after her. She was saddened he did not appear, but her act of slapping him had told him to leave her be. Sparta lowered her head and let more tears fall from her eyes. Her sleeve brushed away the droplets running down her cheeks, and she sniffled in, trying to catch her breath again.

"*Shhh...*" a voice said from behind her as she was grabbed and pulled up from the ground. She felt a blade at her throat and knew this was not Lacedaemon. Sparta could feel herself being pulled back into the bushes and thicket as her feet dragged along the ground. The strong arm around her did not let up or try to be gentle with her.

She was yanked up on a horse and looked around to see a dozen other riders whom she recognized were Thessalian soldiers. Sparta wanted to scream but could feel blood running down her neck from where the blade had pressed onto her skin. The horses began riding, and she felt herself begin to panic.

The man had a hard grip on her, and other soldiers that rode around her gave looks that were threatening. She stayed on the horse and tried her best not to move, out of fear that they would kill her. They traveled a great distance as she kept herself calm and tried to understand why they had kidnapped her. Did they see her with Lacedaemon? Did they know who she was?

Sparta wasn't sure, but she kept her mind sharp and alert. The horses slowed as they reached a camp that was littered with men banging pieces of metal to shape into weapons, practicing battle stances, and discussing the tactics of war. They stared at her intently, every one of them eyeing her. She felt insecure and frightened by all of the wild creatures looking upon her. Like wolves stalking a deer, she was prey in a midst of predators.

The man jumped off the horse and pulled her off of it. He escorted her to a tent, where she entered and stood before a man sitting in a throne. His dark eyes met hers, and his crown was made of gold with red gems that sat on top of his deep, raven-colored hair. The king stared at her intently as his guards remained by his side.

Sparta felt intimidated but tried to remain composed. "Who is this?" he asked softly but sincerely.

"We saw her conversing with the son of Zeus," the soldier who had grabbed her replied.

"Lacedaemon?" the king asked.

"Yes, Your Majesty," the soldier responded.

"Leave us," the king ordered, and all soldiers left the tent, but the guards stayed. The king rose from his throne and looked threatening, dressed in his royal attire. The gold that was laced into

his dark blue robe signified his power, and half of his chest was uncovered. The scars that ran over his right peck and bicep were those from battle, or maybe a beast. Sparta stared at them knowing the man was of great strength if he had survived gashes that deep.

"What is your name?" he asked, rising from his throne.

"Zosime," Sparta replied, knowing she could never give him her real name.

"Zosime. How lovely."

"Thank you."

"Tell me, Zosime. What are you to Lacedaemon?" the king asked, staring her in the eyes. Sparta could feel his breath on her face, and the man's piercing eyes almost looked black. She stared deep within them and thought she could see his soul. Her lips parted to say something, but she stuttered nervously before saying, "I am his whore."

"Really?" he said, surprised.

"Yes," she said quietly. The king looked at his soldiers through the parted fabric of the tent, and they signaled a quiet nod between each other. She was telling the truth according to the soldiers.

"You must be tired and hungry after your journey. Please, allow my servant to escort you to a nice bath and meal," he replied with a smile politely.

"That is very nice of you. Thank you, Your Majesty," she said it with a small bow of respect.

"You may call me Erysichthon," the king said to her as he kissed her hand softly. Sparta smiled as the servant came to escort her out of the tent and to another one. The servant closed the tent tightly, not allowing for anyone to see into it or out of it. She waved Sparta toward the bath, and she reluctantly took off her dress.

The bath was warm, and the servant ringed her hair out of water while rubbing her shoulders. "Do not be fooled by him," she whispered to Sparta.

"I didn't plan on it," Sparta replied.

"You are no whore."

"I am not."

"Who are you really?" the servant asked her.

"It is best if you do not know," Sparta said. She knew the servant could be trusted since she recognized the girl to be a former slave. The rope burns on her wrists and wear of her clothes showed her to be seen as nothing more but a commodity to the king and his soldiers. The girl was here to serve and meet every need that needed to be met.

"You were a slave?" Sparta inquired.

"I still am one. Bought and sold, only to serve," the girl replied, wiping a wet cloth over Sparta's arms.

"I am sorry. What is your name?"

"Helene."

"It is nice to meet you," Sparta said kindly.

"You as well," Helene replied.

"What can you tell me about him, King Erysichthon?"

"It is dangerous to speak of him."

"Tell me, please," Sparta asked her persistently.

"He is unpredictable, charming, cunning, clever, but impulsive and rash. He will try to win you over by swooning you with hospitality. Once he gets what he wants from you, he'll kill you. I've seen him do it with others he's captured," Helene responded, sounding a bit nervous.

"He won't kill me," Sparta replied.

"What makes you think you're any different from the rest?"

"I am a woman. I take it he's only ever captured men?"

"Then, I suppose this is different, but don't underestimate him," Helene said, holding up a towel for Sparta to dry herself with.

"I won't… because I'm going to kill him," Sparta replied.

"How do you plan to do that?"

"I cannot tell you."

"Did you get captured intentionally, in order to kill him?"

"No."

"If you kill him, they'll kill you," Helene said, concerned.

"It is nothing for you to worry about. All that matters is once he's dead, you'll be free, and so will I," Sparta replied confidently.

"You really think you can do it?"

"I'll need your help, and we'll need to trust each other if we're going to survive this."

"You have my trust, but please, be careful," Helene asked pleadingly as she handed Sparta a dress to put on. Sparta nodded her head reassuringly as Helene gave her a plate of food to eat.

Chapter XX

The evening sun had set, and the darkness of the camp was unsettling. The small torches and fires that were lit amongst the tents had soldiers sitting around and drinking out of their cups. They talked small banter and bashed the Dodona army. It made Sparta angry to hear such things, especially how they spoke about Lacedaemon, but she knew he no longer mattered. All that remained important was stopping the war and escaping. If she stopped the war, Laconia along with Dodona would be seen as strong again, and the people would be safe.

She could disappear and be free to live her life how she pleased. All she had to do was kill the king and stop the army. It was a difficult task, but Sparta felt up to it. Helene politely escorted her to King Erysichthon, who was waiting for her at the end of a table.

"Please, sit," he said waving a hand at her. Sparta sat down quietly at the other end of the table, facing the dark king. She could see small candles ignited around the tent to provide light, and his guards stood outside watchfully.

"I know you are not really Lacedaemon's whore," King Erysichthon said, a bit boisterous.

"Then who am I?" Sparta asked, knowing that it was all 'politics,' a game she was learning to play well.

"How about you tell me?" he replied clicking his tongue in his mouth.

"I'm his wife," she said with a smile.

"I had a feeling, as you are much too beautiful to be his

whore."

"Thank you," Sparta replied quietly.

"Why did you lie to me when we first met?" he asked, leaning forward onto the table.

"Because I thought you'd kill me if you knew. Your soldiers were not gentle when bringing me here, and I was quite frightened by them."

"I truly am sorry for that. I have no plans to kill you, Zosime, if that is your name?"

"It is."

"My soldiers told me they saw you arrive on horse earlier today at his side and found you crying under a tree."

"Lacedaemon's?" she asked.

"Yes, him," King Erysichthon replied disgustedly.

"You must've seen us come from the mountains."

"We did. It's quite the battalion you have."

"It's not my battalion."

"You are angry with him."

"Why do you think I was sobbing under a tree?" Sparta said, holding in her pain.

"Tell me, what happened?" he asked curiously.

"He prefers whores to me!" Sparta replied, almost shouting.

"Then you are his loss, Zosime," he responded with sincerity, as he stood to sit in front of her. King Erysichthon brought his head close to hers and once again she could see those piercing embers of eyes. He caressed his hand over her face in an act of comfort and gentleness.

Sparta sat there, not moving but staring at the powerful and enticing man before her. He was tempting her, and she knew it. She moved her head forward to almost kiss him, and as he moved his head forward to meet her lips, she put her finger in between them.

"Forgive me, I do not have it in me," she replied sorrowfully.

"There is no need to ask for my forgiveness. It is understandable that you are not ready for such intimate things," he said, pushing her hair behind her ears.

"I feel I should tell you that his army is no match for yours," Sparta said, still gazing into his eyes.

"I have seen, and you need not to worry. In time, he and all who follow him shall be dead," King Erysichthon replied as he kissed her forehead lightly.

"I am glad to hear that," she said with anger and tears in her eyes.

"Helene!" he shouted as she came running into the tent and then began to say, "Zosime is tired. Please escort her back to her tent."

"Yes, Your Majesty," Helene replied, bowing. Sparta rose as he pulled her into him and once again, kissed her forehead. "You're safe here with me," he said calmly. Sparta looked at him and nodded her head slightly. He let her go, and she followed Helene back to the tent quickly.

The soldiers eyed her from every angle, and she felt nervous. Their eyes ran up and down her body as some smiled, admiring her while thinking about all of the things they wished they could do to her. Sparta was nauseated and wanted to escape this place but knew she must stay. Her tent was ahead, and she saw a soldier with a cup in his hand eyeing her rather intently. He watched her walk all the way into her tent and still stared, even though she was no longer in his view.

Sparta thanked Helene and blew out the candles lit to create light. She laid on the bed and wrapped herself in a blanket. The warmth comforted her, and she found herself feeling calm. Although she was uneasy, she felt safe bundled up in the fort of cloth. The distant voices speaking outside seemed to fade away, and the noise dissipated as Sparta began to let her eyelids close slowly.

The shadows creeped around her and moved in silence amongst the night. A hand fell over her mouth and jerked her onto her back. Sparta tried to scream, but the weight of the hand was too forceful, and she tried to push away whoever was on top of her. She felt the blankets being pulled off her and began scratching at the figure's face, but he only became more determined to make her cooperate.

Sparta could feel a hand running up her leg and thigh. She kicked furiously and, with great effort, bucked her hips to flip the man off her. A scream ripped from her throat that was loud enough to wake the entire army, and she could hear the guards come running toward her tent. The figure stood and lunged at her again, but Sparta kicked and punched harder, determined to get away from the assailant.

She fell from the bed and stood quickly as the shadow figure grabbed her waist and pinned her onto the bed. Sparta clawed to get away and reached for anything she could grab to break herself free of the person trying to harm her. A gurgle sounded from behind her, and she stopped panicking for a moment to listen as something hit the ground.

Sparta no longer felt the forceful arms around her waist and saw light illuminating the tent. She slowly turned around to see King Erysichthon standing before her with his sword covered in crimson blood from the man she recognized as the soldier eyeing her earlier. He was dead on the ground, bleeding out in front of her.

She held her hands over her mouth and quickly fixed her dress as tears fell from her eyes. King Erysichthon handed his sword to one of his guards and pulled Sparta in for a hug. She sobbed and cried into him, scared at what had just occurred. That solider had tried to rape her, and she was thankful he hadn't succeeded.

"You will sleep with me from now on," King Erysichthon said to her, and Sparta did not detest. They walked briskly out of her tent as he ordered his guards to take care of the soldier's body. She clung to him, distraught and afraid, as he hugged her warmly while they walked.

They passed his guards and entered his tent. Sparta wiped away her tears as she entered King Erysichthon's bed. It was much softer than the one she had been laying on, and the blankets were still heated from his warmth before he rose to address the commotion that came from her tent.

"Thank you," she said with tears still streaming down her cheeks.

"You are welcome," he replied, wrapping his arms around her in comfort. Sparta welcomed it, and she nuzzled up to him as he held her tightly. She could hear his heart beat steadily and feel his hand gently rubbing her head. It all seemed to fade away; the fear she felt, the raw emotions running through her, and the anger she felt toward Lacedaemon. Her eyes grew heavy, and she fell into a deep sleep.

King Erysichthon stared at her and smiled admiring the girl's beauty. He watched her steadily breathe in and out as her chest rose and fell. Her hair was soft like her skin, and she smelled of a meadow in spring. It was at this moment that he knew she was different from other women he'd known or even slept with before. This

Zosime was special in a way that put a warmth in his heart and ignited a protectiveness within him. He knew she was never going back to Lacedaemon.

Chapter XXI

Dodona

Lacedaemon watched Sparta run away from him and felt his cheek stinging from that hard slap. He wanted to chase after her but knew he should not. It was time he let her go for once and let her come running back to him. He regretted trying to make her jealous but wanted to confirm that the princess did in fact have feelings for him, just as he did for her.

He touched a hand to his cheek and reluctantly walked back to the building where Callias and Lysander were there waiting for him.

"Their army is mighty in numbers," Callias said to Lacedaemon.

"I do not care how their numbers compare to ours. We still have the advantage," he replied.

"In what way do we have the advantage?" Lysander asked, flicking his hair out of his eyes.

"They are reckless. We are patient," Lacedaemon said to the young boy who could not be more than sixteen.

"Battle is about more than just might; it is about strategy. I understand that now," Lysander replied.

"I'm glad you do," Lacedaemon replied rubbing the emotions, and that slap from Sparta off of him. He carefully listened to the strategies presented by each man and the intel they had gathered on the Thessalian's.

Nicander, Kleon, and Basilius had joined, and all the men sat together discussing the strategy for the battle that was yet to come. The sincerity in their voices and experiences was shared through words of wisdom. The guards and Lacedaemon had fought many battles together, and this would be Lysander's first. The encouragement and training the young kid had received would test his abilities far more than he would ever anticipate, but the thrill of blood being spilled excited him greatly. The stoic guards had reached a conclusion after considerable input was offered and cups of ale were drunk in reward of exhausted efforts to make such a precise plan.

"Apologies for my interruption, but Princess Sparta is not in her chambers," the maiden said with utmost kindness.

"What do you mean? She has not returned?" Lacedaemon asked, concerned.

"I and others have searched everywhere, and we cannot find her," she replied sympathetically. Lacedaemon looked at his guards as everyone quickly rose from the table. They rushed out the door and began searching the entirety of the building, but Sparta was nowhere to be found.

"Check the stables!" Lacedaemon yelled to Kleon, who ran with urgency while he stayed staring at the willow tree. The evening had settled in, and torches were lit to provide light throughout the landscape. He looked at the great tree with regret, and emotions began swirling in his heart. Guilt, remorse, worry, concern, and grief. Had she escaped? Had she run away? She promised him she wouldn't; she gave him her word, but Lacedaemon knew she would not hesitate to break it. It was his fault she was gone.

"Her horse is still there," Kleon said running back to Lacedaemon.

"Then where is she?" Callias asked, confused.

"She ran that way," Lacedaemon said grabbing a torch along

with the rest of his loyal guards. The men set out with ignited sticks in hand to find the missing princess. They asked people they passed by and children who were wandering around. No one had seen her. *Where would she have gone?* Lacedaemon thought to himself.

"Check the fields," he ordered as his guards fanned out to search. The stars were bright amongst the dark night of the sky, and he thought of Sparta. He remembered how they had sat together in the mountains and stared up at the stars together. She spoke of her love for the constellations, and he remembered how the stars sparkling light twinkled in her eyes.

"Over here!" Lysander shouted, and Lacedaemon, along with his guards, ran from each direction toward the voice of Lysander. They reached a tall cypress tree, and Lysander pointed to the drag marks on the ground. Together, the band of men followed the drag marks into the woods.

"Hoof marks. There are many," Callias said.

"I'd say a good number of horses, judging by how many tracks there are along with the spacing between them," Nicander said, sounding intelligent.

"She was taken," Basilius said.

"Callias, take Lysander to the Thessalian camp. Do not engage with them, but watch from a distance. Let me know what you find out immediately!" Lacedaemon ordered.

"If they have her…" Kleon said, without finishing his sentence.

"I know what it means," Lacedaemon replied, frustrated.

Lacedaemon didn't sleep at all that night. He sat under the willow tree and stared up at the stars, hoping—even wishing—that Sparta had not been taken. The stars danced, and he watched as they glimmered high up in the sky. The sun's rays called them back into hiding, and as morning arrived, Callias and Lysander rode on their horses swiftly into Dodona.

"Lacedaemon!" Lysander shouted. Lacedaemon ran over, eager to hear of the news brought by Callias and Lysander, but he could tell by the looks on their faces that the princess was indeed taken by the Thessalians.

"Is she all right?" he asked worriedly.

"She is alive and seems to be treated well. King Erysichthon has shown a fondness for her," Callias replied eagerly.

"That is not good," Lacedaemon replied.

"He has spared her from death. Is that not something we should be thankful for?" Lysander asked curiously.

"He has spared her for now, and we are thankful but for how long he has allowed her to live, I do not know," he responded worriedly.

"Shall we arrange a meeting to get her back?" Callias asked.

"Yes. Send Kleon with a group of soldiers," Lacedaemon responded, and Callias rode with Lysander to the stables as the two quickly ran to give orders to Kleon. He stood there and thought of praying to his father, Zeus, but he knew it was no use. Although Dodona was a sacred place to Lacedaemon and represented a way to communicate with his god of a father, he felt he had already asked enough of him. He would wait for Kleon's return.

Basilius and Nicander tried to console Lacedaemon by distracting him with talk of the battle. The men stood before a table, and everyone carefully studied the field where the battle would occur. They moved pieces over a map drawn by hand with precision. If they were careful and smart, success would be imminently there's.

"Forgive my interruption," a man said, entering the room.

"May we help you?" Nicander asked politely.

"I am a messenger from Laconia," the man replied.

"What news of Laconia?" Lacedaemon asked.

"I think you misunderstand me, as I am not here to bring you news *of* Laconia, I am here to bring you news *from* Laconia," he replied rather boldly.

"You were sent here from Laconia?" Lacedaemon asked.

"Yes."

"What has happened?" Basilius questioned the man, knowing the news he bared was not good.

"I am afraid I bring news of sorrow. The great King Eurotas has died," the man replied.

"How?" Lacedaemon asked, shocked.

"His health had been failing him for a long while... He did not wake from his sleep."

"Who is to rule Laconia?" Basilius asked, a bit upset.

"Queen Clete will take over until they can find an appropriate ruler. You need not to worry," Lacedaemon replied.

"Actually, King Eurotas, in having no sons, declared that upon his death, you would become the king," the man said with a bit of a smile.

"What?" Lacedaemon said, confused at what he was hearing.

"King Eurotas was always fond of you and considered you in many ways like a son to him. You are now the king of Laconia."

"Queen Clete?"

"She will rule Laconia until you return, but you are now the rightful king. I was told to bring you this news and give you...*this*," the man replied, pulling out a gold leaf crown that had a Laconian touch to it.

"I am no king," Lacedaemon replied.

"Yes, you are," the man said, walking over and placing the crown upon Lacedaemon's head before saying, "We are eager for your return to us. May the gods be with you, and may you win this battle," the man walked out of the room, and Lacedaemon was left speechless. He never in his life saw himself as a king but rather as a strong warrior.

Basilius and Nicander stared at him intently before bowing and saying, "Your Majesty."

"You do not need to do that," he replied.

Kleon entered the room, followed by Callias and Lysander. The three men stood and gazed at Lacedaemon, confused. "He has just been declared the king of Laconia," Basilius said, for Lacedaemon who could not speak out of shock.

"King Eurotas is dead?" Kleon asked, confused.

"Yes, he succumbed to illness," Callias replied.

"May his soul rest in peace," Kleon said, sympathizing with everyone.

"Yes," Lysander said, not sure of what to say.

"Your Majesty," Kleon said.

"Please, don't call me that," Lacedaemon said, still uncomfortable with the title.

"I'm afraid we must," Nicander replied with a bit of a laugh. Lacedaemon smiled and knew he had no choice but to embrace his new position. He was a warrior, and now he was a king.

"I bring news of Princess Sparta," Kleon said, interrupting Lacedaemon's thoughts.

"What of her?" he asked.

"King Erysichthon has ordered a meeting between us. We are to meet him when the sun's the highest at the cypress where he took her."

"We will be there. You will all be at my side, and be prepared; he is a nifty king who talks too much. Patience will be needed," Lacedaemon replied to all of his guards, and they swiftly left the room.

He stood there for a moment, taking all in that had happened. Lacedaemon knew he was the son of a god and he had turned himself into a mighty warrior and now a king. The country of Laconia was now his to protect and command. Lacedaemon had inherited great power, but it also meant the risk of winning this battle was all the greater. He could not fail.

Lacedaemon would get back Princess Sparta and kill King Erysichthon on the battle field. He would protect Dodona and defend Laconia at the same time. A king fighting for two countries, and one battle determined the fate of everyone. The crown was light sitting on his head, but the weight it carried in power was unfathomable.

Chapter XXII

Lacedaemon rode on horseback with his guards close to his side. They approached the cypress tree and could see King Erysichthon waiting with guards behind him. The man appeared patient and calm while waiting for them, and Lacedaemon was already agitated.

"Lacedaemon," King Erysichthon said.

"It's King Lacedaemon to you," Kleon interjected.

"Wearing a crown does not make you a king," King Erysichthon replied.

"Where is she?" Lacedaemon asked, fed up with the king's antics.

"She's safe," he said.

"I want to see her," Lacedaemon said bravely. King Erysichthon turned behind to one of his guards, and the guard rode back into the forest. He came back quickly with Sparta, who was on top of a horse of her own.

"See, she is well," King Erysichthon said, almost teasing him.

"Give her back," Lacedaemon said with great authority.

"No. She does not want to go back," he replied.

"You took his wife," Nicander said to the King Erysichthon.

"And now she is mine," he responded coldly with a smile. Lacedaemon looked at Sparta, who appeared to be stern. He couldn't tell if she was afraid, in trouble, or even content.

"She will never be yours," Lacedaemon said bitterly.

"Tell him, Zosime. What do you wish?" King Erysichthon

said looking at Sparta.

'*Zosime*,' Lacedaemon thought, *he doesn't know who she really is.*

"I wish to be King Erysichthon's wife," she replied sincerely.

"No, you do not," Lacedaemon replied.

"To him, I am not a whore," she said, with tears in her eyes that she forced back from falling. Lacedaemon knew she was still angry at him, and perhaps she really did want to be with King Erysichthon.

"I never thought of you like that."

"No, but you love them more than you'll ever love me," Sparta replied, upset, and Lacedaemon knew she was serious.

"King Eurotas is dead. He has declared me the king of Laconia, since he bore no sons to succeed him," he said boldly to Sparta. She looked at him, speechless.

"Really? Well, I'm glad the old man finally passed on. I knew he was hanging on by a thread, but it seems like someone kindly cut it for me. Now, all I'll have to do is kill you, and I'll be the king of Laconia, Dodona, and Thessalia," King Erysichthon said malevolently.

"I'll never let that happen," Lacedaemon replied.

"We are here for Zosime," Kleon said, sternly getting both men back on topic.

"She has already said she wishes to stay with me. I believe she'll make a wonderful queen, don't you think?" King Erysichthon said tauntingly.

Lacedaemon looked at Sparta, who had nothing to offer him but cold eyes. "I will make a great queen of Laconia, Dodona, and Thessalia," she said proudly staring at him.

"Then so be it. Though, I must warn you, King Erysichthon,

you'll have your hands full with her. She's very good at escaping and running away. She even jumped overboard a ship, just to get away from me. Zosime is your problem now," Lacedaemon said blatantly. He could see emotions swirling in Sparta, but she remained composed. She knew he was done with her, once and for all.

"I don't believe she'll be a problem, but thank you for the advice. I'll see you beheaded by my sword soon enough," King Erysichthon replied.

"If I don't behead you first," Lacedaemon said, as he watched Sparta, the king and his guards ride off back into the forest. Sparta looked at him coldly, but he only offered coldness in return. He was done chasing a wild goose that did not want to be caught. It was pointless, and to no longer have to worry about her was a relief in more ways than one.

Lacedaemon turned his horse around as his guards followed him. They entered the stables, and Lysander said, "Are we really letting Princess Sparta go?"

"She is no longer our problem," he replied.

"Your Majesty, that seems a bit harsh," Kleon said, politely.

"It is her own doing, and I am done trying to save something that only wants to run away," he responded, a bit emotional.

"If he kills her?" Nicander asked.

"Then, I am free to pick a wife of my choosing. One who will be easier to maintain," Lacedaemon said, frustrated. Nicander and Kleon looked at the other guards and waved them away subtly.

"I know you don't mean that," Nicander said to Lacedaemon, who was busy unsaddling his horse.

"I do, and I am done with her. I've had enough," he replied angrily.

"So have we, but she is the princess of Laconia," Kleon said.

"And she wanted to run away, escape, jump overboard, and disappear. She has done that, and I hope to never have to see her again,"

"You gave your word," Nicander said sternly.

"And for what?" Lacedaemon yelled, looking at Nicander, before saying, "What was the point?"

"To marry," Kleon interrupted.

"To marry a child who is now a woman who still does not love me?" he yelled.

"I believe she does love you, sire," Nicander said.

"She does not."

"You do not know that," Kleon said, trying to be hopeful.

"Did you not hear what she said? She wishes to be his wife! So, let her be!"

"She could have been lying."

"I do not believe she was."

"What will you do with her when you win the battle?" Nicander asked, worried.

"She has chosen to side with our enemy. Sparta will die," Lacedaemon said, full of hate.

"Your Majesty," Kleon said, before Lacedaemon interjected and said, "Enough! She must die along with all of the Thessalian army and King Erysichthon. It has been decided!"

Chapter XXIII

Thessalia

Sparta gave one last look at Lacedaemon before following King Erysichthon and his guards back into the forest. He meant what he said, and she knew whatever was between them was now over. There was no reconciliation, and her heart weighed heavy in her chest.

The ride back seemed longer than usual, and it left her alone in her mind with thoughts that ran rapid but only brought pain. She had run from him too many times, and Lacedaemon was fed up with her, no, he was 'done with her.'" The man had made that clear as day. Sparta felt emotional and guilty at the same time. She had never made things easy for him, and now, he was the king of her country.

She knew she had a choice. If King Erysichthon won the battle, then she would indefinitely be his queen and rule over Laconia, Dodona, and Thessalia, but if Lacedaemon won, she felt he would kill her for betrayal to her own country. There was no right solution to what her being taken had caused, and she did feel free with King Erysichthon, but on the other hand, Laconia was her country.

Sparta knew she needed to think carefully about what to do. King Erysichthon had also spoken badly of her father, and this did not sit well with her. It meant he hated the royal family, and if he discovered who she really was, he would certainly kill her. She was in a dangerous position and would have to navigate with caution.

They arrived back at the camp, and Sparta dismounted her horse to quickly find Helene.

Sparta ran up to her but was interrupted by King Erysichthon, "Are you all right, Zosime?" he asked with care.

Sparta turned around and said, "I am... not. I would just like to be alone for a moment to process all that just happened."

"That is understandable. I would like to speak with you later over dinner," he replied, walking over to her and placing a hand on her cheek.

"Of course. We will speak then," she said, letting a tear fall from her eye. Sparta felt his gentle hand wipe away the tear that had fallen, and he leaned down to kiss her compassionately on the lips. She was surprised to feel his lips on hers as the kiss came unexpectedly, but she did not pull away from him.

"Until then," King Erysichthon said, pulling away and smiling at her. She smiled in return and looked toward Helene, who seemed concerned. The two walked together down the long line of tents and into the forest. Helene led Sparta to a creek, and the two sat together in the shade under an apple tree.

"What happened?" Helene asked quietly.

"I didn't know he was going to kiss me," Sparta replied.

"He seems quite fond of you."

"It is only because he thinks I'm Lacedaemon's wife and I am now his."

"The son of Zeus? Are you his wife?"

"Not exactly. It's complicated."

"What are we going to do?" Helene asked, biting into an apple, worried.

"Lacedaemon is now King of Laconia. If he wins, he'll believe that I have betrayed Laconia. However, if King Erysichthon wins, then I am queen of Laconia, Dodona, and

Thessalia. There would be peace," Sparta replied, trying to reason with her thoughts that were restless in her head.

"He is not a good king. He is greedy, and he won't stop at Laconia, Dodona, and Thessalia. Erysichthon will try to conquer all of Greece with that insatiable appetite of his, and if given the chance, he will kill anyone who stands in the way."

"You are certain?" Sparta asked.

"I know it with all my heart," Helene replied.

"Then he must be stopped, but I am unsure of how to deal with Lacedaemon."

"Perhaps, there is a way to end this and put you back in good graces with him."

"It runs deeper than that," Sparta said with sadness in her voice.

"Care to share?" Helene asked, kindly handing Sparta an apple.

"He prefers whores to me."

"How so?"

"I saw him with three women, and they were touching him and batting their eyes at him. He didn't even push them away," Sparta said sorrowfully.

"Did he say why he did it?" Helene asked, trying to make sense of the situation.

"He said it meant nothing, but I know he was doing it to make me jealous."

"So, he wanted to make sure you had feelings for him?"

"I suppose, but it made me angry."

"And jealous?" Helene said.

"Yes," Sparta replied.

"I take it that act did not go over well with you?"

"No, it did not. I slapped him in the face."

"You slapped a son of Zeus in the face?" Helene replied, laughing.

"Yes, I did," Sparta said, laughing hard.

"Who are you?"

"I wish I could tell you."

"Me too."

"If Lacedaemon was trying to make you jealous, it means he was looking to see if you felt something for him. Probably because he feels something for you. Although it was wrong how he went about it, I do believe he's in love with you," Helene said, sounding wise.

"I don't know about that," Sparta said, sounding a bit uneasy at that thought, but she had never considered that explanation before. Could Lacedaemon have made her jealous to confirm her feelings for him because he felt for her too? It made sense, but she was unsure if that was the real reason why he did what he did. She thought back to the kiss they shared and knew that he was trying to make her jealous by allowing those whores to touch him. He had wanted her to see him with them. Sparta thought his actions were out of arrogance, but what if they were out of love instead?

The entire situation bothered her, but the openness of this new explanation had made her aware of possibilities she had not considered before. "Thank you," she said to Helene, but was still uncertain about the reality of what Lacedaemon's intentions truly were.

"You're welcome," Helene said.

"What is your plan?" Sparta asked Helene.

"There is a village beyond this creek, and King Erysichthon has not treated them kindly. He has forced them to give up their crops to feed his army and has killed anyone who disobeys. There is talk of revolt against him, but it would take careful planning."

"Even so, a village against an army is not a fair match. The army would slaughter them."

"Other Dodona villages have been pillaged by him too, and they are gathering in the village closest to here. Many have been trained and are ready to fight," Helene replied, hopeful.

"They would never win. The army's numbers are far too great," Sparta responded, concerned.

"I know, but I think now we have a chance."

"What do you mean?"

"You have to trust me," Helene said.

"I trust you," Sparta replied confidently.

"Then you'll need to do exactly as I say."

"I will do exactly what you say," Sparta said, as she and Helene stood to begin walking back to the Thessalian camp. The two spoke intently, and she knew that Helene's plan was a great one, but it would only work if King Erysichthon abided by it. She would have to be careful but knew how to get him to agree.

Chapter XXIV

The evening came quickly, and Sparta found herself sitting across from King Erysichthon as the two ate contently. He sipped his wine, and she ate the plated meal.

"I wanted to thank you for early today," Sparta said, breaking the silence.

"You are welcome. You deserve better than him, and I am just glad that you see 'better' in someone such as myself," he replied, smiling.

"How could I not? You have been nothing but kind to me, and I only hope to please you as a wife but also as a queen."

"You will make a wonderful queen and an even greater wife."

Sparta had finished eating and rose from the table slowly.

"Is everything all right?" King Erysichthon asked, concerned as to why she was getting up. Sparta did not answer, but walked over to him and sat in his lap. She gazed into his dark eyes and kissed him tenderly. King Erysichthon welcomed the kiss eagerly, and Sparta felt the warmth of his lips on hers. She pulled away to say, "Everything is more than all right, but I am worried."

"About what?" he asked, still fixated on her.

"My former husband is stronger than you think, and I want you to win."

"You doubt me?"

"No, I just want you to return alive to me," Sparta said, kissing him again.

"I shall return to you. You do not need to worry," King Erysichthon said to her, kissing her back.

"What if he captures me again?" she asked, breaking their kiss.

"I will never allow that to happen."

"How can you be certain?"

"Because we will win."

"What if he or his guards tries to find me? How will you keep me safe?" Sparta asked, acting afraid.

"You will be safe," King Erysichthon said to her, reassuringly.

"How?"

"You will leave."

"And go where?"

"Someplace far away from here that is safe."

"Your palace?"

"Yes."

"And I will be safe there?"

"You are the future queen of Laconia, Dodona, and Thessalia. We need to make sure that you are protected in order to bear future heirs, and there is no place safer than my palace," He said with hopeful eyes and sympathy at the same time.

"Future heirs?" she said with a smile before saying, "You wish to have children with me?"

"Someone will need to inherit all we conquer," he replied before kissing her intimately. Sparta could feel him running his hands down her waist contently, and his tongue caressed hers as they shared a passionate moment together. She ran her hands through his hair and pulled away, gently smiling at him. He smiled back, and she said, "When must I leave?"

"Morning," King Erysichthon replied.

"What if they see me?" Sparta asked, acting worried. King Erysichthon sat for a moment before saying, "You shall leave tonight in the dark of the night. They won't see you, and it'll be safest."

"Are you sure?" she asked him, looking a bit sad.

"Yes," he replied as he began to kiss her again.

"If you feel that is what is safest for me, then I will leave tonight."

"Guards!" King Erysichthon yelled, and they came running into the tent. "Prepare a small number of well-trained soldiers to escort Queen Zosime to my palace safely. You will all leave tonight," he ordered, and the guards left with haste to meet his request.

Sparta kissed him passionately again and said, "I wish we had more time."

"You will see me again, and we will have all the time in the world," he replied.

"May Helene come with me?"

"She may. You will need a woman to attend to you."

"Thank you."

"You are welcome."

"Your Majesty, everything is ready just as you've requested," the guard said, interrupting them.

Sparta looked at him reluctantly and appeared to be full of sadness. King Erysichthon looked at her and said, "My Zosime. We will see one another again."

"I know, I'm just going to miss you," she replied with a smile of love.

"And I shall miss you," he said kissing her again before standing. Sparta got off his lap, and the guard escorted them both outside. A small band of horses with a dozen soldiers sat at the ready with Helene. Sparta looked at King Erysichthon once more, and he said, "Do not worry. This will all be over soon." He kissed her again and looked at her lovingly. She hugged him tenderly, and he gently guided her up onto her horse.

They began marching off through the tents and into the forest. Sparta glanced once more, back at King Erysichthon, and she could see solace in his eyes. The man truly did care about her, but she knew his empathy would be over the second he figured out who she really was. He also had no respect for her father or for her country.

King Erysichthon was on a quest of power, and he would do whatever was necessary to achieve it. Sparta knew her duty to her country came first, and despite Lacedaemon becoming king, she still felt obligated to help her people. She was the Princess of Laconia after all, and no one would ever take that away from her, not even a son of Zeus.

Helene's plan had worked, and the soldiers willingly led them through the forest and across the small creek. The moon's light gleamed from above and showed shadows dancing all around them. An owl hooted in the distance, and bats flew overhead catching bugs. The night was quiet and tranquil, as the soldiers remained vigilant.

They had trotted on horseback for some time, and a small village appeared in the distance. The fires lit on torches and in circles on the ground ignited the buildings with light as shadows danced up and down. All was quiet as they marched through the town, but that was just as Helene said it would be.

The soldiers had made it outside of the town and to the edge of the fields when one soldier suddenly fell to the ground. Another fell after him as the horses began to panic. Sparta held onto the reigns of her horse tightly as Helene looked at her, offering trust. Another soldier fell to the ground, and the rest rose their shields around themselves and Sparta.

They all at once began running at full speed to evade whatever had killed the other soldiers. A "thud" from behind, and another solider fell onto the ground dead. His body rolled in the field as they continued riding faster. They rode through the trees, and Helene had described it as a labyrinth with paths that crossed in every direction. It was an easy place to get lost or disoriented.

The soldiers stopped with a halt, and Sparta sat in the middle of them with Helene at her side. An arrow stuck one soldier in the eye, and he fell from his horse, another fell from an arrow in his back and Sparta turned to see another drop to the ground with a dagger in his back. One soldier was about to say something but was interrupted by a spear hurtled through his chest. The man fell to the ground, and the horses ran off, afraid.

The remaining four soldiers looked confused and could not tell from which direction the arrows or weapons were coming from. Another arrow pierced one of the soldiers in the heart, and

Another jumped off his horse. He wandered through the thicket of trees, but a blade struck his core. The last two stayed close to Sparta and Helene. They drew their shields and swords close, but both met their death with an axe.

Sparta and Helene sat on top of their horses and did not move. The dead men around them made Sparta nauseous, but she refrained from looking at them. A woman with her hair tightly wrapped in a braid rode on a white horse. She waltzed over to Helene and said, "She must be important if they sent this many with her."

"She is," Helene replied with a smile.

"Follow us," the woman said.

A band of women emerged from the forest, and Sparta

watched as they began tending to the dead soldiers' bodies. She and Helene followed the woman through the thicket and maze of trees to a building at the bottom of a hill that was hidden by dense woods. The river flowed with great force, and Sparta could see a bridge ahead, but they were not crossing it. They veered to the building, and the woman dismounted her horse.

"You want to tell us who you really are?" the woman said.

"You are not Zosime, that's for sure," Helene replied.

"How do I know you won't kill me?" Sparta asked, concerned.

"You don't," the woman replied sternly.

"I am Princess Sparta of Laconia," she said, taking a risk that the woman would not kill her.

"Princess Sparta of Laconia is dead," the woman replied.

"No, I am alive," Sparta responded, preparing herself to tell the story of her survival again.

"She died in a 'sailor's doom,'" Helene said.

"I was rescued by sirens and stranded on a bank of sand for four years."

"Really?" the woman replied, not believing Sparta.

"It was punishment for running away."

"Running away from what?" Helene asked, confused.

"I was only thirteen and did not wish to marry Lacedaemon," Sparta replied.

"You ran away from marrying Lacedaemon, the son of Zeus?" the woman said, shocked.

"Yes."

"And you survived the wreck because sirens saved you? You were there for four years?" Helene asked.

"Yes."

"How did you survive?"

"The sirens taught me how."

"How did you get off the land flat?" the woman asked.

"Nerissa, a siren, and her sisters dragged me into the ocean, where Lacedaemon 'rescued me' and took me to Ithaca," Sparta replied.

"Did he know it was you?" Helene asked, now enticed in the story.

"No, the longer I was with the sirens on that piece of sand, the more memory I would lose. It wasn't until we were in Ithaca that I realized and remembered everything."

"So, you're alive, and Lacedaemon knows?" the woman asked, confused.

"Yes, and he wasn't too happy about it at first, but overtime, I think he liked me more. As much as I tried to escape from him, he never gave up on chasing me," Sparta said, remembering the past.

"Things are no longer well between you two?"

"No, I'm afraid not."

"It's not entirely her fault," Helene said, vouching for Sparta.

"I'm Apollonia," the woman said.

"Pleasure to meet you," Sparta replied.

"Well, Princess, it seems we have much to prepare for and very little time."

"I will explain more to you about her when we get inside," Helene said to Apollonia. Both women shook their heads in acknowledgement that Sparta had been through much and needed to rest. Helene knew Apollonia would need to know what happened between Sparta and Lacedaemon to understand how to best navigate the battle that lay ahead.

Sparta fell asleep on a pile of blankets in the building as

Helene and Apollonia talked quietly outside. She wasn't sure if Apollonia fully trusted her or not, but she had nothing to lose. Laconia was hers to fight for, and she would do whatever was necessary to protect it from King Erysichthon, and even Lacedaemon, if she had to.

Chapter XXV

The sun was bright, and the clouds moved with the wind in the sky. Sparta had come to learn that Apollonia was a former slave of King Erysichthon's. She had escaped and vowed revenge against him for all he did to her. The woman was in her late twenties, and her emerald green eyes were piercing. The black charcoal under them showed her fierceness, and the former slave had turned herself into a mighty warrior.

Helene and Apollonia had survived King Erysichthon together, and although Helene could not be freed as fast as Apollonia, the two never forgot about one another. They had been planning a revolt for years in secrecy. Sparta had come to respect both of them immensely, and even though she was a princess who was not warrior like, she knew she would have to be.

She remembered watching the guards train in Laconia and thought of the brave men in the colosseum slaying beasts fearlessly. Sparta had always wanted to be able to do that, but she was shunned from ever having thoughts like that. Queen Clete had taught her composure, grace, and elegance. Sparta was all of those things but wanted to be more.

Apollonia stood with a stick in one hand and a shield in the other. She explained to Sparta and Helene how to hold them and began teaching the women how to use them. The stick took swift motions in Sparta's hand, and Helene caught on easily. "Swing left, swing right, strike straight, strike left, strike right. Shield steady," Apollonia said.

*

Sparta seemed to get the hang of it and was proud at how fast she was learning. Apollonia began whacking her stick against Sparta's and the two engaged in combat. Helene watched and then took a turn for herself against Apollonia, who proved to be a worthy opponent. When it was Sparta's turn again, she wanted to try something different. She remembered the guards' moves in Laconia, and when Apollonia charged her again, she swiftly maneuvered her stick and pinned Apollonia to the ground.

"Where did you learn to do that?" Apollonia asked, stunned.

"I remember watching the guards train in Laconia," Sparta said with confidence.

"You are going to make a great warrior," she replied with a smile, and Helene stepped in to begin training again. The women trained together for some time and shared laughter amongst themselves.

With each passing day, Sparta and Helene grew stronger like Apollonia. They could hold their own, and when soldiers from the village came to participate, both Sparta and Helene put them on their knees. The women had grown into warriors, and every day that the battle did not occur was another day they trained for the day it came.

Apollonia had taught them how to use a bow and arrow, throw daggers, use axes, and to use objects around them as weapons. She taught them all there was to know about battle, and Sparta brought the wisdom of strategy to the table. Both Apollonia and Helene were always amazed at how much Sparta knew of timing and tactics.

The sun had set, and it had been three months since she had

left King Erysichthon's camp. For the first time in her life, Sparta truly felt free and confident in the power she held. She placed her hand on her sword like she had seen Lacedaemon do before and understood that it was a stance of confidence rather than intimidation, but it could be assumed as one or the other.

The women slept peaceful but were awoken by a soldier who was in great disarray.

"Thessalians are gathering at Dodona as we speak," he said with panic in his voice.

"Ready our soldiers and horses. We leave at once," Apollonia replied, and the man rushed out quickly on his feet.

"Are you both ready?" Apollonia asked, turning to Helene and Sparta.

"Yes," both answered at the same time. Apollonia dressed in her armor, as did Helene and Sparta. They carried their shields on their backs and had daggers at their sides. Sparta had preferred her sword on her back than placed at her side. It seemed easier to fight that way for her.

The women traveled over the bridge and walked down a path to climb up a small hill. Together, they stood and stared at the soldiers who had gathered from villages around Dodona; some even came from Thessalia, as they did not agree with what King Erysichthon was doing. The soldiers were not in the slightest small in numbers, like Helene had told her.

Sparta stared at the immense number of men and women who stood before her in the hundreds, if not thousands. She smiled, knowing there was hope after all and today would be the day she would save Laconia, Dodona, and Thessalia.

The sun had begun to rise, and its light was low, but enough to see through the darkness that was night. Sparta mounted her horse as Apollonia and Helene did the same.

"Think you forgot this," Apollonia said, placing a gold leaf crown on top of Sparta's head with care. Sparta smiled, and Helene smiled, knowing that this was the day they would all rise to seek vengeance. "You should say something," Helene said to Sparta.

"They know who you are. That's why so many people are here. We had spread the word quietly," Apollonia said to Sparta.

Sparta stared at the army before her and said, "I, Princess Sparta of Laconia, am the daughter of the great King Eurotas, daughter of the valiant Queen Clete, sister of Tiasa, and rightful ruler of Laconia. I survived the impossible and have traveled far to save my country and yours from King Erysichthon. We gather here together as one to defend everyone that we love and to protect all that we hold dear to our hearts: our families, our friends, and our countries. Today, we fight for them, and we fight for all. I will lead you into battle, and if I die, know that I died for you. I died for Laconia, Dodona, Thessalia, and its people. May we fight with valor, and may the gods be in our favor!"

The army cheered, and they began marching to the battle field. Sparta, Helene, and Apollonia had memorized the entire terrain of where the battle would take place. There was nothing they did not know, and had rehearsed every scenario possible. Helene knew how King Erysichthon fought, and Sparta had learned how he thought.

In the short time she spent with him, she knew the man would be reckless just as Lacedaemon had told her. He relied on numbers as his advantage, but his strategy was weak. She knew Lacedaemon was a man of logic, and his tactics would be fearsome. He was strong and stoic in every way, and fighting alongside her father had taught him everything he needed to know about battle and more.

They reached the hill and stood there, shielded from the view by a line of trees. The massive field of jade green grass swayed in the wind as both armies stood there, opposing each other.

King Erysichthon's army was massive in numbers and was bigger than Lacedaemon's army, but Sparta knew numbers meant nothing. It was how you used them that mattered.

Sparta, Apollonia, and Helene would wait for the right moment to introduce themselves. They did not want to provoke or escalate things more than they already were. The tension was high and could be sensed by everyone as both armies stood patiently awaiting one or the other to strike first. *It's a game*, Sparta thought, but one she knew, she could win. She was no longer the princess who was weak or dainty. Her time with Apollonia and Helene had turned her into a fearsome warrior, and she felt closer to that of a queen.

She held herself high on her horse, and behind her heard the distant crunching of footsteps. Sparta turned around to see even more soldiers falling in line behind them. "If they could not join us at the village, they were to join us here. We sent messengers to summon them; the instant we heard Thessalians were gathering at the battle field," Apollonia said to Sparta, who stared in disbelief at the number of soldiers behind her. This was more than an army; it was a militia of great quantity, and she was sure that she had more soldiers than both Lacedaemon and King Erysichthon combined.

Sparta looked at Apollonia and Helene, who looked at her with encouragement. The armies were about to move when Sparta rode her horse out beyond the tree line, showing herself to all. Helene and Apollonia were at her side, and Sparta sat on her horse, staring down from the hill at both armies. She could see everyone looking at her intently, but the distance was so great that she wondered if King Erysichthon or Lacedaemon could see her at all. The armies had halted from attacking and seemed confused at their presence.

Sparta had wanted them to be wondering what she was doing here. She wanted both armies to be caught off guard. As the armies stared at her, Sparta lifted her sword from its sheath and raised it high above her head. Helene and Apollonia did the same. The soldiers slowly came out from behind them, and both armies could see that they were here for battle.

Helene rode back into the forest, and Apollonia charged down the hill with a number of soldiers on horses behind her. Soldiers spilled down the hill on foot after her, and Sparta stayed steady on her horse. A great number of soldiers were gathered behind Apollonia as she conquered the middle of the battlefield. They did not attack but raised their shields and spears in preparation of King Erysichthon's army.

Sparta stood on the hill and lowered her sword. A number of soldiers came from behind her and raised their bow and arrows, ready to fire. A soldier handed Sparta a bow and an arrow. She was done waiting for someone to strike first. Helene and Apollonia knew it was her who needed to make the first move, declaring war. Sparta held an arrow lit with fire and released it into the air. It landed hitting King Erysichthon's shield, and his army advanced with a ferocity.

The men began running eagerly toward Apollonia and her battalion, but they held steady. They did not move, and Sparta and her soldiers released a flurry of arrows from the hilltop. The arrows rained down from the sky and hit many of King Erysichthon's soldiers.

Chapter XXVI

Dodona

Lacedaemon had woken up early and received news that King Erysichthon and his army were gathering on the battlefield. Kleon awaited his command, and together, they rallied the other guards and soldiers to begin the journey to the war. The men got ready quickly, and Lacedaemon mounted his horse. He had sharpened his sword every day in anticipation of cutting King Erysichthon's head from his body.

The past few months had not been easy for him; he thought of Sparta every day and how much he wished he could go back and change what happened between them. He had experienced anger and frustration the first few weeks without her, but it quickly turned into sadness. She was with another king, who was dangerous and unpredictable. He couldn't protect her or save her if King Erysichthon decided to kill her.

His thoughts wouldn't leave him, and he only hoped that she was somehow still alive. He knew he may never win her back, and he had been rash with his words toward her. The princess was his to marry and love, but he had failed at both of these things. He knew deep down he cared for her more than he should, given the predicament they were both in. If she really had betrayed her country and really was King Erysichthon's wife, then he must kill her.

He could not hesitate or stutter in any way. It is his duty to protect Laconia, and the crown came first above all. Lacedaemon did not like being a king, but had accepted that he must live up to the potential and the power he had been given. He would stop at nothing to protect Dodona,

Laconia, and its peoples. His bravery would serve him well, and he would let his sword strike down his enemies. He felt battle-ready.

They arrived at the field that was covered in a plain of grass, and he could see King Erysichthon's army. It was greater than he had imagined, and the soldiers were lined in rows neatly. He could see catapults ready to launch with boulders and the shimmering helmets that covered each soldier's head.

"This is greater than what we planned for," Nicander said to Lacedaemon.

"It is, but we still have the upper hand. They are reckless, and King Erysichthon would rather wager numbers than use actual strategy. He is a fool for thinking numbers will win him victory," Lacedaemon replied, faithful but hesitant.

"Everything is ready," Callias said to Lacedaemon, who nodded in reply and watched as Callias, Basilius, and Kleon rode back into the forest. Lysander stood with the army, and Lacedaemon sat on top of his horse, with Nicander standing on foot next to him.

The tension in the air was heavy as Lacedaemon waited for the army to strike. He knew King Erysichthon was an impatient man and would make the first move. The two stared at each other from across the battlefield, and hatred filled Lacedaemon's veins. The army began to move but suddenly stopped.

"What is that?" Lysander asked, referring to an armored figure on horseback sitting perched at the top of the hill. Lacedaemon and his army shifted their focus to the hill to the left of them and watched as two other armored figures emerged. They were far away, and he could not make out their faces but could see that one was wearing a crown.

"Who are they?" Nicander asked.

"I have no idea," Lacedaemon replied, confused. The three figures sat on their horses, and the one with the crown drew a sword, and the other two drew theirs as soldiers began appearing behind them. One armored figure charged down the hill as the soldiers on horses followed behind, and then more men on foot. The other armored figure had turned back into the forest, but the one on the hill wearing the crown stayed there, watching everything.

This battalion, led by the armored figure on a horse, he realized was a woman with blonde hair, kept tightly in a braid. She sat on her horse behind a wall of men with shields and spears pointed in between them. The rest of the soldiers on horses had bows and arrows at their ready, and behind them were more soldiers ready with swords and shields. It was a strong formation, and they looked fearsome, standing in front of Lacedaemon and his army as they faced King Erysichthon's mighty fleet of men.

Lacedaemon stared, confused, with his men and guards as to what was going on. King Erysichthon and his army looked just as confused. He watched as more soldiers emerged from behind the armored figure with the crown. The figure put their sword away and was handed a bow and arrow. He watched as it was lit on fire and the arrow was shot directly at King Erysichthon. It hit his shield, but Lacedaemon knew it was a threat and an act of provocation.

He watched as King Erysichthon's army charged forth, and as they ran toward the battalion, a blizzard of arrows released from the hill. He watched as they hit the soldiers running toward the blonde woman's army. The soldiers on the hill reloaded their arrows and fired again, letting arrows rain down. The battalion stood firm; they did not move, and they did not flinch.

Lacedaemon was impressed, and Kleon had emerged from the forest. "Who are they?" he asked, confused.

"I have no idea, but tell the archers to begin firing from the trees onto King Erysichthon's men who are charging at them," Lacedaemon ordered. He couldn't explain it, but he felt these strangers, who had formed a battalion in front his army, were friends. They continued to fire down arrows from the hill, hitting the Thessalian soldiers. The woman with the blonde hair signaled for her archers on horses to release their arrows, and more men fell dead onto the grass below.

Another wave of soldiers were released by King Erysichthon, and yet the archers kept firing, hitting more and more men. It seemed almost effortless, as not a single person had yet, got their sword bloodied. However, Lacedaemon saw the catapults being loaded, and he knew it would soon be a massacre of the battalion and his army.

He was about to give Nicander a command when he saw the figure in the crown on the hill launch a flaming arrow into the Thessalian army. Lacedaemon was confused as to what that did, but he saw the ropes of the catapult begin to burn, and he smiled greatly. He watched as the figure in the crown released another arrow full of flame and hit the second catapult before it could launch. The rope burned, and both catapults sat there useless.

Lacedaemon looked up once more at the figure wearing the crown and realized why it felt so familiar. *Could that really be Sparta?* he thought to himself and felt a flush of hope run through his body with excitement. If it was her, she hadn't betrayed her country after all, and he smiled at the possibility of that thought.

Kleon and the guards had ordered the archers to release a wave of arrows from the trees, which rained down on King

Erysichthon's army. The girl with the blonde braided hair looked back at Lacedaemon and smiled. He smiled back, knowing they were here to help him. The victory of archery did not last long as King Erysichthon's anger had hit its high. He ordered his entire army to charge forth and Lacedaemon ordered his army to stand with the battalion in front of them.

The crowned figure on the hill continued to release arrows with soldiers from above to lessen the impact; the force of the soldiers hitting the battalion and Lacedaemon's army would have. Together, the battalion and the army stood there in unison as one united front. All were prepared to fight to their deaths, and all were ready for blood to be spilled onto their swords.

King Erysichthon's army hit forcefully, but many of his soldiers pierced the spears first and were trampled in the effort to reach Lacedaemon and the battalion. The raid of arrows continued to fire down from above. The girl with the blonde hair looked at Lacedaemon and smiled. He knew something was about to happen; he just didn't know what.

"Hold the line!" the girl shouted. "Do not let them break it. Hold steady!" she ordered, and the soldiers stood.

"Step back!" Lacedaemon ordered, getting off his horse and said again, "Step back." His army stepped back in unison as the battalion stepped back while still holding the line. He could hear the screams before he could see what was going on. The attention of King Erysichthon's army had turned from them and onto what was coming from behind.

The girl with the blonde hair looked at him again and yelled, "He's foolish to think we'd only attack from the front," and Lacedaemon knew what she meant. The other armored girl with the dark hair had rode back into the forest to lead another group of soldiers to attack from behind. He now understood their plan, and it was brilliant, but he knew the strategy all too well.

It was a tactic used by King Eurotas, and he knew the figure in the crown upon the hill was indeed Sparta.

King Erysichthon's army had no choice but to try to run up the hill she was perched on, and Sparta quickly led a fleet of soldiers down the hill to crash into his army. They made a wave that split the Thessalian army in two, and she whipped out her sword to begin carving the way to victory. The battalion quickly began fighting the soldiers as Lacedaemon's army followed them onto the battlefield.

Lacedaemon could hear King Erysichthon calling his name, and he boldly walked toward the man while cutting down Thessalian soldiers like trees. He had reached King Erysichthon, and as he lifted his sword to battle the reckless king, he saw a sword being jabbed through king's torso. The King of Thessalia fell to the ground, and the girl with the dark hair stood in his place as she drew her sword up and swiftly brought it down to behead him.

Chapter XXVII

The girl with the dark hair looked up at him, and Lacedaemon nodded his head in thanks. He looked to the left to see Sparta striking down soldiers left and right. She was alive, and he was in awe of what he was seeing. He struck down soldiers that tried to whack him as he made his way over to her.

She turned around to hit him with her sword, but he quickly blocked it in defense. Sparta stared at him, and he smiled at her. She smiled back and lifted her sword to impale a man behind him. Lacedaemon snapped back into focus, and his guards joined him on the battlefield.

"Sparta?" Lysander said, stunned.

"It's Queen Sparta to you," the girl with the blonde hair said, as the other girl with dark hair followed behind her. Together, Lacedaemon, Sparta, the guards, and the two women who he'd come to learn as Apollonia and Helene, stood in unison, fighting the last of King Erysichthon's army.

They worked as one, and their armor glimmered as the sun had fully emerged into the sky. Its rays bounced off their swords and shields that were wet with blood, and when the last Thessalian soldier was killed, they all breathed a breath of relief. They looked at each other, proud of what they had accomplished together. The kingdoms and countries of Laconia and Dodona were now safe. They had won the battle that would be talked about for centuries to come.

The armies cheered in victory as Helene held up King Erysichthon's crown, proud of the vengeance she had acquired.

The battle was won, and everyone went back victorious to Dodona. Sparta rode on her horse ahead of Lacedaemon and his guards, with Helene and Apollonia at her side. He could tell she was no longer the girl she had been three months ago, and he knew she had earned the right to be called a queen.

The people cheered with celebration as flower petals were thrown and thanks were given. The exhausted army, soldiers, and guards sat at the tables filled with food to celebrate the accomplishment. Sparta had dismounted her horse, and Lacedaemon desperately wanted to talk to her, but she was swept away by Helene and Apollonia.

"You need to eat," Kleon said to him, and Lacedaemon followed his guards into the building to have a private feast. They had bathed, and ate until their stomachs hurt. "The Great King Lacedaemon has led us to victory," Nicander said, standing up toasting to Lacedaemon.

"I am afraid I am not the one we should be raising a cup to. Princess Sparta... Queen Sparta, is the one who assured our victory with the help of her friends. We drink to them," he said with thanks in his voice and everyone raised a chalice to salute the three powerful women. It was when the feasting was over, that Lacedaemon left to take a moment to breathe.

He left the building and went outside to hear boisterous laughter coming from other buildings and children dancing on the road. All was well, and everyone was happy tonight. He looked up at the stars as they shined brightly in the night sky. The wind blew across his face, and he looked over to the willow tree that moved with the breeze. Sparta was there, sitting under it, and he smiled, staring at her.

Lacedaemon walked over and asked, "May I join you?"

"You may," she replied, as he sat down next to her, leaning

against the large tree.

"Stars are quite beautiful tonight," he said, trying to make conversation.

"They are beautiful every night," Sparta said, smiling and staring up at them.

"Thank you for what you did today," Lacedaemon said to her kindly.

"Laconia is my home, and its people are my people. I would do anything to ensure its protection."

"Who taught you how to fight like that?"

"Apollonia."

"Really?"

"Yes."

"You fought well."

"I know...thank you."

"Who are your friends to King Erysichthon?"

"Helene and Apollonia were his former slaves. Apollonia escaped before Helene, and the two have been planning a revolt for years. I am thankful I was the one to lead it. I couldn't have saved Laconia, or Dodona, and even Thessalia without them," Sparta said, sounding grateful.

"They seem like great friends," Lacedaemon replied.

"They truly are. Helene and I formed a plan to convince King Erysichthon that I would be safer at his palace than at his camp. He bought into it and let us go," Sparta told Lacedaemon.

"I'm glad, and I'm thankful to know that you did not mean what you said that day we all met at the cypress tree," Lacedaemon replied.

"I could never be his wife. I would've killed him first if Helene hadn't gotten there before me."

"It seemed as though you wanted to be his wife."

"I am supposed to be your wife, remember?"

"I do," Lacedaemon answered, smiling at Sparta, who smiled back.

"If I catch you with a whore again, I will behead her," Sparta said, teasing him.

"I don't doubt you, but you need not worry about that. I was just trying to make you jealous, and it was foolish on my part," Lacedaemon said, with apology in his voice.

"To try to see if I had feelings for you?" Sparta asked.

"Yes."

"You could've just asked me."

"That seemed a bit forward, and given that you ran away to Cythera, lived on a flat of sand for four years, jumped overboard into waters with a sea serpent, and climbed through a window while scaling down a building, all in order to not marry me. It did not seem so simple of an ask," Lacedaemon replied with a laugh.

Sparta laughed and leaned over to kiss him. "You're right, I probably would've slapped you if you had asked me how I felt about you," she said laughing. Lacedaemon smiled and kissed her back gently. Her lips were warm and sweet, just as they had been the first time he kissed her under the willow tree months ago. He placed his arm around her waist, and Sparta ran a hand through his hair. She climbed onto this lap and allowed herself to feel his lips against hers.

The noises of celebration faded into the background, and it seemed the world around them had slowed. It felt as if just the two of them existed and no one else. Sparta continued to kiss Lacedaemon tenderly, and he embraced her with all his heart. She pulled away to look at him and smiled before saying, "I'm sorry for running away."

"Don't be. You've taken me on quite an adventure, and I've

enjoyed the ride," he replied, smiling.

"Even though I made it difficult for you?"

"'Challenging' is a better word, but I have never been a man afraid of a challenge."

"You're persistent enough."

"My persistence made me a king."

"The king of Laconia."

"And you are the queen of Laconia."

"I have to be coronated first, and we must be wed."

"Yes, we have much to do," Lacedaemon said running his hand over Sparta's cheek and smiling at the thought of finally being able to marry her. Sparta kissed him, and the two curled up under the willow tree, watching the stars together. She fell asleep in his arms, and he stroked her

hair gently. He took one last look at the stars, and thanked his father for the blessing he had taken for granted. Then, he closed his eyes and fell asleep.

Chapter XXVIII

Two Years Later...

Lacedaemon stood on the palace's terrace, overlooking the ocean, and watched the boats in the bay. He held his son, Amyclas, in his arms, and the little boy laughed, trying to pull off the crown from his father's head. "One day it'll be yours, but not today," Lacedaemon said to him, and he laughed contagiously.

He smiled and looked at his son, who had his dark brown hair with little curls spiraling at the ends and the stunning blue-green eyes of Sparta. The boy was going to be just as charming as him and just as clever as his mother. Lacedaemon knew with their guidance, that their son would someday become a great king, and he looked back at the ocean in awe of all the boy would inherit one day.

Since his return to Laconia, the people had named Lacedaemon their "savior," and decided to rename the entire country after him. It was no longer Laconia; it was now known as "Lacedaemon." He was not in favor of the change in name, but he would grow into it the same way he had grown into being a king.

It suited him well, and peace was restored. All was just as it should have been.

"Daydreaming again?" Sparta asked, as she joined him on the terrace with their newborn daughter in her arms.

"Always," he replied, kissing her.

Sparta smiled and said, "My mother and father would be

proud."

"They would be very proud of you," he replied.

"They would both be proud of *us*," Sparta corrected.

Her return to Laconia had the people in confusion, but they recognized the young girl in the woman she had become. The celebrations were grand, and everyone was astonished at how their Princess Sparta had returned to them. She told her story that would be passed along for generations to come, and everyone would know about her grandness.

Queen Clete had passed away shortly before she and Lacedaemon had arrived back at the palace. The maidens had informed Sparta that her mother had not taken the loss of her father well, and they suspected that she died of a broken heart. Sparta had her mother buried next to her father and sister, Tiasa.

In the years that Sparta was gone, Tiasa had fallen pregnant and died in childbirth. Her parents believed that they had lost both daughters, and the kingdom only felt right to be handed to Lacedaemon. After all he had done for them—for the country and the palace—that man had earned the right to be the king.

Though her family had passed on, Sparta had made her own. The marriage between her and Lacedaemon was a union that solidified an era of peace. She felt confident, leaving Helene to rule Thessalia with Kleon. The two had grown exceptionally close, and both were trusted friends of her and Lacedaemon.

Apollonia was always a warrior first and an explorer second. She was never afraid to travel where she was called to, and never shied away from a fight. The girl was untamable until she met General Adamantios. The bond they shared over the battle, and the blood being shed solidified them as not only the generals of the Lacedaemonian Army but also in marriage. Their wit and boldness made them an unstoppable force, and Sparta was glad to have them close to her.

Lacedaemon's guards had moved up in the ranks and earned the positions they deserved. Nicander was the commander of the new guards and took it upon himself to train them whom he saw fit. He liked teaching them battle tactics and watching their eagerness to serve and fight. The job was one that made him smile, and he sought it an opportunity to pass years of wisdom onto the young men. He also felt a sense of pride in knowing he'd be training the next generation of protectors and guards for the kingdom and the country.

The young Lysander had grown into an impressive soldier and an even more impressive naval commander. He had found his calling, and the way he commanded ships made Lacedaemon proud. His strategy was extravagant and unique, but always claimed victory. The young man always returned to the kingdom and told great tales of the countries he helped to defend.

Callias and Basilius had found a new venture, and together they remained heroes of the Colosseum. They battled strange beasts and even men, slaying them every time without failure. Sparta and Lacedaemon were always in the audience to cheer the brave men on, and they took great pride in looking danger in the eye and winning.

Lacedaemon did miss the days of glory, but he had found a new form of it in Sparta and their children. He kissed his newborn daughter Eurydice's head, and smiled at her intently. The small newborn was quick to offer a grin back, and he only hoped that when it was her time to find a husband, she would not be so bold or adventurous to run away as Sparta.

He knew he would do things differently and would make sure it was a match that was more than politics, but one that also consisted of love. Sparta smiled at Lacedaemon and said, "The new city, how is it fairing?"

"I have placed it by the river, and I believe it will prosper immensely," he replied, smiling.

"I am eager to see it," Sparta said, as the breeze moved her hair gently. She smelled the blooming flowers of jasmine and daisies that were blossoming in fields all around. The wind had carried its scent right to the palace, and she thought of the willow tree.

After her return, she had gone to see it. It was the place where she was honored and memorialized by her family and people. The kindness of it brought tears to her eyes, and she remembered staring up at the great willow tree that she used to climb as a child. It had become their son's favorite tree, and although he was still a bit wobbly in his legs, she had no doubt he would grow into them. It was only a matter of time before her or Lacedaemon would be climbing up the tree to yank him out of it, just as her father had to do with her many times.

"I know you will like it," Lacedaemon replied to her, snapping her out of the memories.

"What have you decided to name it?" she asked him.

"It will be a glorious city, and that means it can only have the most glorious name."

"And what is that?"

"Sparta," he replied, smiling. She smiled back happy at the name, and the two stood there together, holding their children, dreaming of the life they would grow up to lead, and how

someday, all of that would be there's to rule. *For power is within us all*, she thought, and hoped that one day their children would both be brave enough to find it.